The
Devil's
Missal

Cathy Dobson

**Grosvenor House
Publishing Limited**

This book is published by
Grosvenor House Publishing Ltd
Link House
140 The Broadway, Tolworth, Surrey, KT6 7HT.
www.grosvenorhousepublishing.co.uk

This book is a work of fiction. Any resemblance to
people or events, past or present, is purely coincidental.

A CIP record for this book
is available from the British Library

ISBN 978-1-78623-551-0

For Chris, Maddy, Nathan and Alice

Acknowledgements

They say addiction runs in families. It was my dad who introduced me to reading. He had been hooked on reading for years, just like his own father. His daily route home from the office to Piccadilly station in 1970s Manchester took him past Gibbs second hand bookshop – though walking past the shop was something he rarely did. At least twice a week he'd arrive home with one of their carrier bags dangling next to his briefcase. He read constantly; on the train, in his armchair, in bed, sometimes even at the tea-table to my mother's horror. His general knowledge was encyclopaedic. My mother read too but she had far less time to devote to books. Reading for her had to be slotted in between her busy medical practice, the demands of the family, the garden, Scottish dancing, knitting, sewing, lacemaking and a hundred other things. She taught me to be selective about what to read.

So, I blame both of my late parents for my book habit and for the fact that my house is so full of their books that there's barely space for anything else. Apart from cats. There is always space for cats.

When I went to Cambridge it never crossed my mind that I would read medieval literature. The seeds of that obsession were laid by Elsa Strietman, an inspirational Dutch lecturer in the curiously named "Department of

Other Languages." Elsa could bring any long-dead author to life with her vivid descriptions and stories. Under her charismatic tutelage, history became tangible. You could see, taste and smell the places where the authors had lived. Her devotion to the Middle Ages sparked a lifelong love affair with the period in many of her students, including me.

When I moved to Germany, our family moved every couple of years until we discovered Meerbusch. This cluster of villages nestling by the Rhine quickly became home to my husband, myself and our three children. Our first six years were spent living in Schloss Pesch, a two hundred year old manor house which has the potential to spark a thousand stories. We later moved seven kilometres south to Meerbusch-Büderich to an old, dilapidated farmhouse near the edge of the forest. I would like to thank everyone in Meerbusch for your wonderfully warm welcome. I am delighted to have been able to join you now as a fellow citizen.

I would never have got this far without the help of some wonderful supporters. I can only mention some of the main contributors here. Suze St. Maur, who has been a constant friend, advocate and provider of sound advice and encouragement. The ladies of the Boudoir, who kept me encouraged and buoyed my mood whenever I was starting to flag. Claire Jennison, who slogged through the first complete draft and suggested a radical change to the chapter sequence which I thought wouldn't work until I tried it. Claire also provided valuable relationship guidance to Holda and Rupert and prevented their liaison from going awry at a crucial moment. In addition Claire proofread the entire document, corrected all my errors and pretended to me that there had hardly been any. Angela Gilmour combined her outstanding creativity and disturbing cupboard full of black magic artefacts ("I'm sure I've got a human skull lying around somewhere...") to shoot the cover photo. Angela also inspired many of the positive feminist vibes in the book in more ways than she'd probably want me to explain here.

Last but definitely not least, the greatest thanks of all go to my wonderful, supportive husband Chris and my three amazing children, Madeleine, Nathan and Alice, without whom the book would probably have been published six months earlier.

I should finally like to point out that *The Devil's Missal* is a work of fiction. Any accidental similarities to historical events, or people living or dead, are purely coincidental.

Prologue

As the day of the lecture drew nearer, Professor Holda Weisel, the eminent Rhineland medievalist at Düsseldorf University, found herself struggling for only the second time in her life, with writer's block. When she had received the invitation from the Royal Institution in London to give that year's prestigious Christmas lecture her heart had leapt. This flagship media event would be televised live by the British Broadcasting Corporation and the rights syndicated to over a hundred television and new media channels around the world. Holda had recognized at once what an honour this invitation was and replied immediately, accepting it.

But now, whenever she sat down to start her script, her mind seemed to go blank and she was left staring at an empty screen. Only one story seemed to want to formulate itself in her brain, and that story she wanted at all costs to suppress.

As the deadline loomed, she felt her resolve weakening. Something deep within her, a terrifying memory she had been smothering for two decades, was stirring in her subconscious. Hideous flashbacks and horrid visions kept her awake at night. Her beloved academic themes retreated to some part of her brain that was out of reach. Her life seemed reduced to a desperate struggle against one malignant memory.

With only two days to go before the live screening, Holda gave in. She dragged aside a low bookshelf in her study and hacked furiously with a knife at a particular part of the wallpaper behind it. The thin plasterboard yielded to reveal a hidden niche. From that hiding place, Holda retrieved an old yellow letter and a hard drive of the sort that used to be found in laptops two decades before. She slotted it into the special adapter she'd always kept and watched as the old images appeared on her screen. Then sitting down at her keyboard she began to type frantically, as though she were possessed.

Two days later, as the cameras began to roll on her scandalous Christmas lecture, which would almost cost the BBC its charter, she remembered the inauspicious evening twenty years earlier which had launched her academic career.

Chapter 1

I've got to start somewhere. This PhD thesis plan won't write itself, typed Holda, scowling at her laptop screen as once again the right words failed to formulate in her brain. Her gaze drifted to the window of her room in the house she shared with four other post-graduate students, where the last of the lilac blossoms were flapping in the wind as though driving the very thoughts from her mind. A lone magpie flapped gawkily across the sky. Beyond, the ancient gate tower of an old Cambridge college rose up against a dull sky. Holda could see darker clouds mounting on the horizon.

If I could only get the first sentence down, she agonised, then maybe the words would flow. But her fingers hung motionless above the keyboard. Her brain refused to transmit anything other than a numb paralysis to her digits.

It will be pouring with rain when I walk round to college for supper, thought Holda in an effort to distract her mind from its stupor, but even being soaked will be better than staying in this stuffy room, getting nowhere with my research. Why did I ever think a doctorate in medieval German literature was a good idea anyway?

A ding emitted from the machine and a tiny alert in the corner of the screen caught her eye. It was an email from Professor Azriel Finster, her Director of Studies at the Cambridge University Faculty of Modern and Medieval Languages. A gaunt, aloof man, with whom

Holda had so far had few interactions and who she found strangely intimidating. An email from him was about the last thing Holda needed right then.

The message was a curt instruction to present herself at the professor's rooms in the neighbouring college, at eight that evening.

He doesn't phrase it as a question, thought Holda, he already knows I don't have anything else to do tonight. Where else would I be, apart from staring at this screen and trying to muster a coherent sentence? I hope he doesn't want to see a first draft of my thesis yet.

As a reluctant concession to the upcoming meeting Holda changed into her only jeans which weren't ripped at the knees, a baggy white shirt and a pair of pink sneakers. She pulled a brush through her shoulder-length chestnut hair and scowled back at her skinny image in the mirror on the back of her wardrobe door. She looked like a starving cat with her tapering face and too-large green eyes.

"Well what can he expect on what the university pays me?" she mouthed sharply at her reflection. She worked her arms into a too-tight khaki parka bought at a charity shop, stuffed a small notepad and pen into its pocket and then, checking for her keys, she let the room door click shut behind her and strode quickly down the stairs and out onto the wet street.

Dinner in the Jacobean dining hall was sparsely attended and the food that evening mercifully uninspiring: chicken, potatoes and peas. It was Holda's only meal of the day and she wanted something unchallenging. She sat a little apart from the other graduate students, working at her meal intently, systematically, fearful that if she made eye contact someone would ask how her research was going, for want of anything better to say.

They're all so much brainier than me, she thought, none of them has ever spent an afternoon in front of a blank screen. They're all brimming with great ideas and momentous theories. I'm the only one here who can't even string a sentence together. Whatever would my parents have thought if they could see me now?

The jolt of that thought made her drop her fork onto her plate with a clatter. There was a momentary hush as what seemed like a hundred faces turned to stare at Holda. Then, as she blushed furiously, the hundred faces displayed synchronised indifference by returning seamlessly to their conversations and their dinners.

Holda's parents, both classicists, had been killed in a car accident near Heidelberg six months previously while on their way to an academic conference. Those six months since the news came in were still a blur. Holda fancied she had spent the majority of that time lying on the sofa staring at the ceiling.

Of course, she might have delayed starting her doctorate under the circumstances but she had already been accepted to the research position, and had actually been awarded funding. Admittedly, it was only a tiny grant but still as rare as hen's teeth in her academic discipline. It was not something she dared let slip from her grasp. She had prayed that research into medieval German manuscripts, which she normally found all-absorbing, might take her mind off her bereavement. No, bereavement wasn't the right word; she wasn't grieving in the generally accepted sense - that would imply that she felt something at all. Holda was just numb. Her mind repelled all attempts at thought. She was like a hollow shade ghosting around the university, observing the world through a veil.

It wasn't even as though she'd had much to do with her parents in the last five years. Her teenage phase had ended turbulently. Her parents had made it known how disappointed they were in certain choices she had made. Their main gripe had been her downright refusal to take Latin and Greek in the sixth form. When she had chosen to study German at university it was almost by mutual consent that they had drifted into a sullen estrangement. And that distance had become permanent. There had been no way back.

Once everything's sorted out, thought Holda, things will be easier. Once probate has gone through and the house is sold there will be money at least. Money will mean choices, alternatives, possibilities. But in her heart she knew that money or lack of it wasn't the problem. Something had broken inside Holda. She could never get back to her old, intact, early childhood self. There would always be chips and cracks and rough edges. She was like a porcelain bowl which once rang melodiously when tapped but now, being damaged, would only emit a dull clunk.

She finished eating and noticed with a start that it was already time to set off for Professor Azriel Finster's rooms in the next-door college. Noiselessly, she pushed back her chair and stole out of the dining hall.

It wasn't quite dark yet on the streets, but the steely clouds and driving rain made it feel pitch black already.

Holda pulled the hood of her parka round her face and began to jog along the pavement as close to the lee of the college wall as she could. Before she reached the corner her blue jeans and pink sneakers were sodden and muddy. Three minutes later, as she launched herself through the door at the bottom of Professor Finster's staircase, water was streaming down her face and body and already forming a puddle on the tiled floor at her feet. As the heavy door swung shut behind her with a bang, she leaned against it for a moment, panting in the darkness. She pushed back her parka hood, brushed some strands of wet hair back from her face and then reached for the light switch. Before her finger made contact with the button, however, the staircase was suddenly flooded with light and the gaunt, dark figure of Professor Azriel Finster was leaning over the bannister above her.

He was a tall, pale man of around fifty-five with thick, black hair swept back to the nape of his neck. He wore a neat, black beard showing a few streaks of grey. His eyes were deep set and intense and so dark that Holda could not tell the colour. He was smartly attired in a black collarless shirt, black jeans and expensive looking black leather boots.

"Rain is a great leveller Miss Weisel," he remarked. "It bathes all of our faces in streaming tears."

That's just the sort of thing he always says, thought Holda. Something enigmatic which you can't even reply to. Even his name, Finster, means dark and obscure in German.

"I seem to have made a bit of a puddle on your floor," she stuttered and felt her cheeks redden.

"No matter. The lady who cleans will attend to it tomorrow morning, if it is still there. Hang your coat on the bannister where it can drip safely, and come upstairs to the fire."

Holda did as he instructed and soon found herself sitting on a battered leather armchair in front of an ancient two-bar electric fire, which gave off an oddly metallic smell. The only lighting in the room was a single desk lamp by the window, and the red glow of the electric bars.

"May I offer you a glass of wine?"

Though nominally phrased as a question, the professor's tone left no option of refusal, nor did he wait for a reply before pressing a glass of ruby liquid into her hand. Holda thanked him in a voice which seemed even reedier than her normal tone, and sipped it apprehensively. The wine warmed her without affording relaxation. She wondered what was coming next.

The professor seated himself in the armchair opposite her at the other side of the fire, his back to the light on the desk. To Holda he was a black silhouette. The crimson light from the fire barely lit his features, except the whites of his eyes which glowed red. Her face, in contrast, was fully illuminated by the lamplight.

"How are you getting along with your research?"

So this is it, groaned Holda inwardly. He's found out somehow that I've produced nothing and he's going to throw me out of the university.

"Fine," she lied. "I'm just finalising my thesis plan. I should have something to show you…next week." Her voice foundered. She wondered how blatantly obvious the bluff was.

The two red hollows narrowed and the professor's silence compelled Holda to go on speaking.

"The last couple of days didn't go so well," she found herself confessing. "Writer's block or something I suppose. I couldn't seem to formulate the words. But I'm sure it's only temporary. I'll get something to you in the next day or two."

The professor sipped at his wine slowly.

Is he savouring the wine or the taste of my misery? Holda wondered. The seconds of silence ticked by unbearably.

"I have a proposal to make to you, Miss Weisel," the professor announced suddenly. "Or may I call you Holda? An unusual name."

"It's not my actual name. I chose it myself. My parents called me Aphrodite. They were both classicists…but I couldn't go through school called that. I was at primary school in Germany. The other children turned it into 'Affe', which means monkey, and made chimp noises at me…" Her voice tailed off and her eyes pricked.

"But you chose an old Germanic name for yourself? Holda, meaning beloved."

Holda nodded, not trusting herself to speak.

"I assume the name turned out to be appropriate?"

Holda closed her eyes, feeling two fat, tell-tale tears squeeze between her lashes and sear a trail down her cheeks. She had never for one moment felt love for herself, even as a child.

"My parents spoke only Latin to me when I was growing up," she blurted out. "They read me Greek and Roman mythology at bedtime. I was supposed to become a classical scholar like them. My parents are dead now…" Her voice tailed off.

The professor made an odd sound which might have been a chuckle.

"Well Holda, I wholly approve of your choice. You may call me Azriel, a name which I fear lacks such aspirational premeditation as yours."

He paused while they both took another sip of wine. Then he announced suddenly, "Holda, I have a proposal for you."

Here it comes, thought Holda. He's trying to put it nicely but he's about to fire the bullet. She shut her eyes. Her shoulders slumped.

"I have an important task for you."

Holda's head jerked up in surprise.

"I need you to travel to Germany to investigate a manuscript which has recently come to light. It is a matter of the utmost urgency and secrecy. You will need to get there this week. Tomorrow if you can manage it. I can arrange to have your teaching taken care of for the rest of the term. We can't afford to wait the eight weeks until the long vacation starts. There is no time to lose."

Holda's mouth fell open and it took a few moments before she remembered to breathe. Questions jostled with each other in her brain. Finally one found its way to her tongue.

"What manuscript is this?" Then, as he did not reply immediately, "Why is it so urgent, Azriel?"

As she spoke his name she seemed to taste the odd, burning, metallic flavour of the electric fire in her mouth.

Azriel Finster stood up, reached for the wine bottle from the mantelpiece and topped up both of their glasses. Seating himself again he began to speak.

"The manuscript is a medieval bound book. I don't know its exact date but if it's what I hope it is, I estimate it originated in around the 1360s. It was discovered last week during renovation work in the chapel of an old aristocratic manor house in the Rhineland. It was concealed inside a lead box which had been bricked up in a hollow recess in the chapel wall. It is a set of parchment, or possibly vellum, documents bound together into a book. Some of the writings appear to be in Latin and some in Middle High German. Without seeing it myself, I cannot say whether it is the original work of the scribe or a copy."

He paused, took another long draught of his wine and continued.

"From the inscription in the front of the document, it seems that it may contain original texts by Johannes von Deibel, a medieval scholar whose life work was, until now, thought to have been lost. I have learned much about his work from other learned contemporaries and later scholars. It is of critical importance that we evaluate this document before any of the German universities find out about its existence. Right now we are the only people who know about it…or at least who know of its significance."

But I don't know of its significance, thought Holda anxiously. Am I supposed to have heard of Johannes von Deibel? Why should I have to go and see this document? I don't know anything about this subject.

"Who was Johannes von Deibel?" asked Holda.

The red eyes flared for a second, as though they had been opened wide and the fire reflected off the whites. Azriel continued speaking.

"I first came across the story of Johannes von Deibel in a lengthy set of marginalia in a religious manuscript held by the Diocese of Aachen. The story of von Deibel's origin is a strange and gruesome one, jotted down in Middle High German by one of the novices in the scriptorium of the monastery of St. Suitbert in Kaiserswerth. In parts it was difficult to decipher as the ink was badly faded, but here is what I learned: this young monk was scribbling down the story of one of his contemporaries in the margin of an otherwise unremarkable religious tract. His notes related to a certain brother named Quirinus. At the time their order was a strict, contemplative one. Some of the brothers spent entire months or years in retreat, locked in their cells, receiving meals through a hatch in the door, and engaged only in contemplation and prayer. It would appear that Quirinus was one of these recluses. This fact alone made what happened next so inexplicable to his fellow brothers. Quirinus, while locked in his cell for more than a year and apparently never leaving it, contrived to give birth to a baby boy."

"Quirinus was really a woman!" exclaimed Holda.

"Not quite," answered the crisp voice from the shaded face opposite. "On examination it was found that Quirinus was possessed of a complete set of male genitalia. But he also had all the female reproductive organs. He...or she...was what used to be called a hermaphrodite. Nowadays we would say intersex."

"But if he...I mean she...was locked in a cell, how did she get pregnant?"

There was a pause on the other side of the fireplace.

Then Azriel explained, "There are two possible theories, Holda. One is that Quirinus was not as secluded as was supposed. Perhaps he had contact, for example, with a father confessor or with other brothers, for instance in the infirmary. The marginalia only give us the novice's version of what Quirinus told of the events. That account was quite possibly extracted under torture. According to Quirinus, the pregnancy came about as a result of him masturbating in his cell and then manually inserting sperm into his own vagina. Quirinus claimed to be both the boy's mother and his father."

"Is that even possible?" asked Holda, astonished.

"I checked with my colleagues in the biology department - quite technically it is. But it is equally plausible that Quirinus made up the story to protect another monk, who was his lover. At this remove we will probably never know."

He's relishing telling this tale, thought Holda. He's observing my face as he crafts each sentence. He's savouring my every expression and picking his words to elicit surprise, shock, disgust. He's testing me. But for what?

"So what happened to Quirinus and the baby boy?" she inquired, struggling to keep her face inscrutable.

"The church authorities judged Quirinus's physical abnormalities and pregnancy to be the result of him having intercourse with the devil. He was allowed to remain in his cell and nurse the baby for a year. After that, the child was removed and the cell bricked up, leaving Quirinus inside to starve to death."

Despite herself, Holda sensed an icy shudder run up her spine.

"How horrible! Oh God!" she exclaimed, recoiling. "What did they do with the poor baby?"

The black outline opposite her shifted almost gleefully against the lamplight. Azriel had got the reaction he wanted out of her. The red eyes constricted as though he might be grinning at her. She wished she could see his face properly. She needed to know whether his expression was mischievous amusement or something altogether more sinister. Her whole body was taut; all her senses straining to catch his next movement or sentence.

"The infant they named Johannes von Deibel – literally John of the Devil – and they tried to bring him up in the monastery to be a monk. He seems to have been an exceptionally clever child who learned to read and write early, and studied extensively in the monastery library. But perhaps as a result of his name, or the reputation which attached to him from his birth, he appears to have strayed from the ways of the Benedictine order. He was eventually banished from the monastery and there our marginalia scribe loses touch with him."

"Was he ever heard of again?"

"There are several references to his writings in esoteric texts of the period. Our young devil clearly made quite a name for himself among the more heretical and occult fringes of religious thought. But none of his actual texts seemed to have survived. By 1486 when the Malleus Maleficarum was written by the Dominican friars, Kramer and Sprenger, von Deibel's work seems to have been virtually forgotten. As you know, the Malleus Maleficarum became the basis for all subsequent witch trials, and was the authority used by the Inquisition. By the time it was written, Johannes von Deibel had clearly sunk into obscurity. The discovery last week of this manuscript, bricked into the chapel wall at Schloss Pesch in Meerbusch, may be our chance to resurrect him."

Holda felt another shock jolt through her body. Schloss Pesch? That was the old yellow mansion in the trees, set back from the road near Ossum. She had spent her early childhood near there. She even had played in its overgrown park as a girl. They had moved away to England when Holda was ten and Pater had been awarded a classics chair at Cambridge.

How does he know? she thought urgently to herself. How can he possibly know? I never told anyone about Schloss Pesch. Somehow he has learned about my childhood history.

"Why do you think the manuscript is written by Johannes von Deibel?"

The red eyes contracted and then widened again.

"I can't be absolutely sure. That is what I need you to find out. Go to Meerbusch, examine the manuscript and email me with your findings. You read Latin and Middle High German fluently. You can find out what is written there and send me a transcript and a translation of it. For the moment it is stored in the town archives in Meerbusch-Büderich. The archivist is a puffed up jobs-worth called Rupert Keller, who flatly refuses either to photocopy it or to send me the original to inspect. The fool can't read Latin or Middle High German well enough to evaluate it himself. Frankly, I'd be surprised if he can sign his own name. Technically, I can't leave Cambridge until July. However, if the document does turn out to be what I think it is, I will somehow manage to fly over and join you in Meerbusch and we will work on it together. Until then, here is enough money for your journey and expenses for the next three weeks. Also a note with details on how to contact Keller. I've booked you into a quiet, family hotel near the town hall.

Again – the details are in the note. Let me know if you need anything else."

Azriel handed her a thick, sealed envelope.

Then, as though it were an afterthought, he added, "I trust this won't interfere with any personal plans you may have. Am I right that you are single?"

"Yes," answered Holda quietly. "I've always been single."

Even if I don't want to go, I can't refuse him, thought Holda. Firstly, because he's my Director of Studies and can influence whether I stay at Cambridge or have to leave. But mostly, because he exerts a power over me which I can't put into words. He understands things about me that he shouldn't be able to know: that I'd be available this evening, that my thesis plan isn't going well. He knows about the schloss, he knows I speak Latin as well as medieval German. How could anyone have known that?

"So you will be able to set off immediately, Holda?"

"Of course," she announced. "I can leave first thing tomorrow morning."

Chapter 2

It was still dark when Holda slipped out of the shared house and stomped through the chilly air, across the park to the city bus station. She had a heavy holdall slung over her shoulder containing most of her clothes, her laptop and some blank exercise books. Azriel's envelope was tucked into the inside pocket of her parka. She caught a bus to Trumpington and made her way up the high street, to an imposing sandy coloured house behind a high wall. Holda slipped through the wooden gate quickly, and noiselessly let herself into the house with a latchkey. Her parents' house.

Holda shivered and not just because the heating was off in the empty building. Everything was still exactly as it had been on the day of the funeral, except that a film of dust had settled over the entire house.

They haven't left yet, Holda thought. Their presence is impressed into the pattern of the wallpaper. The whole house smells of them and their old books and queer ways. They are here, watching for something or someone. It's so quiet I can sense the silence pushing down on me, suffocating me. I never could breathe freely in their house.

She made her way quickly upstairs into what had been Mater's study. She deliberately left the door wide open, not because she needed an escape route but because the urn containing the ashes of her parents was sitting next to Mater's diaries on the shelf behind it.

She was supposed to scatter the ashes secretly at some archaeological site in Greece in the summer. Holda did not want to think about that right now. Instead, she turned on the computer on the desk and the printer next to it. The brightness of the screen seemed incongruous in that spectral house. Holda gritted her teeth and focused on her mission.

In the next twenty minutes she booked a trip over the Dartford Crossing, a one-way ferry journey from Dover to Dunkirk, and printed off directions from Trumpington to Meerbusch in the German Rhineland.

I must get myself my own printer, she thought. Then, with a shudder, she realised that as soon as probate was settled it would be her printer, and her computer and her desk. Not that desk, she thought. Not that computer or printer. I need my own stuff. Mater hasn't relinquished her things, she's inside them. Both my parents are everywhere here. I mustn't let them overwrite me again. I have to create my own story.

The house watched silently as she closed everything down again, pulled out all the plugs, extracted a set of car keys and insurance documents from her mother's desk drawer and left the building, locking the door behind her. Then she made her way swiftly to the double garage at the back of the house. Inside stood Mater's battered, old, black Volkswagen. The space next to it was ominously empty. Her parents had taken Pater's car when they set off on their last fateful journey towards Heidelberg.

Holda felt another tremor along her spine, quickly stashed her holdall on the back seat and got in. She hoped the battery hadn't gone flat in the four weeks since she had last gone round to borrow the vehicle.

Luck was on her side. The engine started on the second attempt. She reversed out, leaving the motor running while she closed the garage door.

Do they haunt the car as well as the house? Holda wondered. As she eased herself into the vehicle she checked the glove compartment. There she discovered her mother's reading glasses and a well-thumbed anthology of Ovid's love poems. How typical of her, thought Holda. The car radio has been broken for a decade but, instead of getting it mended, Mater just read Ovid in any traffic jam. Holda got back out and put both items into the dustbin by the side of the garage.

"You're both of you to stay here," she called out fiercely, surprising herself at the sudden loudness of her own voice in the morning stillness. "Mater, Pater, you're not coming with me on this trip." Then she returned to the car and set off towards the motorway. The house watched her until she was out of sight.

As Holda put distance between herself and Trumpington she felt her mood lift. She could legitimately leave all thoughts of her PhD thesis aside for the next couple of weeks and focus on this new task. As she considered it though, her brow wrinkled.

I'm really not well prepared for this at all, she realised. I don't know anything about this Johannes von Deibel. That weird story of Azriel's about his intersex parent doesn't explain anything at all about him. I mean about what he was like, how he lived, what he studied, why he was considered influential. Azriel didn't tell me the truth about why it's so urgent either. It surely can't be to do with academic rivalry. He must know something about von Deibel's work that he isn't letting on.

Holda pulled in at a service station to refuel the car. She bought herself a bottle of water and a packet of sandwiches.

"Take care in all the traffic going south today," advised a gloomy, puffy-faced man behind the till. "There are some real idiots on the road nowadays. They all drive too fast and half of them are on their mobiles at the same time."

"I know. I'll watch out," replied Holda. That's exactly what killed my parents, she added inside her head.

Despite this unpropitious exchange, when she got underway again she felt decidedly cheerful. Whatever happens, it's an adventure anyhow, she told herself. I shall think of it as a medieval quest. I'm galloping off into the unknown in search of...of...what exactly? Her brain flicked through the various medieval stories she had pored over during her academic studies, through all the fairy tales and legends she had read. Pater would say it was the Golden Fleece I was looking for. Mater would have me as Psyche wandering the world looking for Cupid. But this quest isn't about treasure or love. Johannes von Deibel doesn't sound loved or lovable. And it's not the manuscript itself that's valuable, it's the information in it that interests Azriel. Could that be the Holy Grail I'm seeking? Does it contain some form of enlightenment? Or perhaps there's a damsel in distress or a handsome prince or a buried treasure that I don't even know about yet. Maybe the manuscript is just a literary artifice created by a deus ex machina to kick-start my story. Perhaps the real quest is for something different. If I were writing this story I'd make myself into a hobbit and have my quest lead to a magic ring that makes me invisible. Holda smiled at the thought but then a cloud flitted over her features. But I am already invisible to most people, she thought. Then she asked aloud, "Is Azriel dictating my story now?"

The orbital motorway around London was less of a snarl-up than Holda or the gloomy oracle at the service station had feared. The traffic was heavy but mostly it kept moving. Holda weaved the little Volkswagen deftly between the heavy goods vehicles and told herself that she was navigating a labyrinthine forest full of dragons and ogres. Turn-off signs were ominous forks and cross-roads which could lead her away from her quest into unknown peril. Then, an hour later, the road swept her upwards onto the Dartford Crossing and she imagined she was driving across a rainbow above the glittering Thames. My quest beats Mater's Ovid into a cocked hat, she thought defiantly. Who needs a car radio anyway when you've got an over-active imagination?

Soon after that Holda turned off the London orbital following signs for Dover.

"This is the chosen path," she pronounced out loud, then laughed at her own melodrama. But seriously, she thought suddenly, why had she agreed to go on this journey? Why hadn't she quizzed Azriel more about it? She remembered the ill-lit room of last night, her professor's black outline and mysterious demeanour, and her cheerful mood began to seep away.

I should turn around now, she thought. There's something unreal about all of this. I'm driving myself to an unknown destiny. But do I have the option to back out now? What if it ends badly? What if my destiny is death on the road, just like happened to Mater and Pater?

Yet still Holda kept on following the signs towards Dover.

If the quest was supposed to cast labyrinths or monsters in her path, it failed. Holda made good speed and reached Dover two hours earlier than the ferry she'd reserved a place on.

"I can change your booking onto the earlier crossing if you like," offered the cheery check-in clerk after tapping vigorously at his keyboard for a few seconds. "There's one sailing in ten minutes – you'll just have time. There's bad weather brewing from the west later so you'd do well to get ahead of that."

Holda acquiesced gratefully and drove round to where the last line of waiting vehicles was beginning to move in single file up the ramp, and into the maw of the cavernous ferry.

On any sea voyage, even one as mundane as a cross-channel car ferry, it is difficult to focus on your destination until you have lost sight of the land. So it was with Holda. She stood apart from the other passengers on the blusteriest part of the top deck, with her eyes screwed up against the scouring of the spray, as the Kent coast slowly retreated. With it receded her Cambridge College, her unwritten thesis, Professor Azriel Finster, her parents' house, the urn, Ovid and all the other things which had hung over Holda like a storm cloud.

When she could see nothing but a grey line of horizon where the slate sea met the colourless sky, she turned. On the other side of the ship the coast of Europe had materialised, equally grey and misty, but to Holda that shore beckoned with mysterious and alluring possibilities.

She moved indoors to the deck below and ate her service station sandwiches. They tasted stale. At the other end of her table was a couple in their twenties with a little girl of about three. The girl was on her father's lap and he was reading her a board book with holes in. As he poked his fingers through the holes they completed the book's illustrations to form the bodies of worms and caterpillars. The child giggled helplessly at each page as though she were being mercilessly tickled.

"Read it again!" she shrieked as he closed the book at last. "Read the wriggly wiggly worms again."

"We've had that one five times now, petal. Let's read the new book I just bought you instead."

"There are princesses in the new one," added the girl's mother encouragingly. "Worms are icky."

The girl's face crumpled to a defiant pout and she clutched the board book close to her chest. "I want the wriggly wiggly worms again."

The girl's mother looked across at Holda with a semi-apologetic grimace as though trying to enlist support. Holda evaded her glance deftly and stared at her own lap.

Don't give in, she urged the girl from inside her own head. Insist on your wriggly wiggly worms. Don't let them take your story from you. If they do, you won't ever hear it again and you'll always have to read their books and be their little princess. Stand firm. Make them read you your wriggly wiggly worms.

Holda got up, which caused the little girl to notice her for the first time.

"Wriggly wiggly worms are the best worms," Holda remarked.

The little girl beamed at her and held up one hand, waggling all her fingers. Holda grinned back, wondering with a momentary shock how long it was since her face had stretched those particular muscles.

"Never ever stop wriggling," she urged, suddenly serious, and then walked away to find the restrooms, leaving the young family staring after her.

They actually noticed me, she thought to herself. Since I started on this journey, I'm becoming visible.

It was early afternoon when they docked in Dunkirk, and the mass of drivers and passengers filed down to the car decks to reclaim their vehicles. Getting the earlier ferry had put Holda two hours ahead of her self-imposed schedule. She only had to make it to Meerbusch by late evening after all. She couldn't go in search of the disagreeable Rupert Keller before the archive opened tomorrow. As she sat in her car waiting to disembark, she studied the map she'd printed out. She listed the towns she'd pass on the way: Bruges, Ghent, Antwerp, Eindhoven, Venlo, Krefeld.

I'll make a stop at Bruges, she thought. I'll park up and stretch my legs for an hour. There's no point in arriving in Meerbusch too early.

An hour later she found herself off the motorway and navigating the ring road around Bruges. She parked near an imposing medieval gate and walked into the old town.

Bruges is a medieval scholar's dream, thought Holda. It is complete, original and breathtakingly beautiful. It still looks just as it would have done when it was built in the late middle ages. It spans the gothic and renaissance periods. Look at the buildings bristling with stepped gables, embellished facades, statues tucked into niches and everywhere little turrets, finials, mouldings and gargoyles. Of course, when the river silted up at the

end of the middle ages the whole town slid into disrepair, suspended in time like a foetus in formaldehyde.
Old buildings with their brickwork disintegrating,
flaking slowly and inexorably away, and no money to
repair or replace anything.

As Holda stepped through the old stone gate of the
town she felt as though a magic turnstile had trans-
ported her back in time. The narrow cobbled streets
were all but deserted at that hour, and she turned
instinctively away from the wider shop-lined thorough-
fare to lose herself in the labyrinth of residential alley-
ways. Tiny terraced houses hunched themselves
comfortably together, as they had done for centuries,
their facades weathered, their seasoned brickwork
pocked with the passing of time. Some sported a growth
of ivy or clematis which seemed the only thing holding
the bricks together. Somewhere close at hand church
bells were ringing, the notes tumbling through the air
like falling leaves. Further on someone was roasting
meat and the scent of it hung on the air. Later she passed
a little cloister with a herb garden facing the road, all
neat, little, geometric beds surrounded by clipped box
hedges. A carillon in the distance began to ring out a
stuttering folksy melody.

It was on streets like these that Johannes von Deibel
lived, thought Holda. In houses just like these. He
would have recognised all these herbs and known their
properties and powers. He would have heard church
bells like this and understood the message they con-
veyed. But his streets would have been packed with
people and animals. There would have been knitters
and lace makers sitting on doorsteps, playing children
clattering up and down in wooden clogs. There would

have been crying babies, barking dogs, clucking chickens and crowing roosters. There would have been horses and donkeys hauling carts over the cobbles. Laundry would have flapped on ropes slung between the houses. Street vendors would have shouted out their wares. There would have been lay preachers, town criers and entertainers, all yelling for attention. There would have been filth and noise and smells; a real hotchpotch of odours from cooking and wood fires, breweries and tanneries and, of course, everybody's excrement. Chamber pots would have been emptied into the streets. Horse dung, dog faeces, chicken droppings would all have been lying in steaming heaps where they landed. What I'm seeing now is just a ghost town. No, not even that. Even phantoms don't inhabit Bruges any more. It's as though the living are the ghouls now, the zombies. It's so uncannily empty, silent, lifeless…

A harsh whirring noise, which seemed to be getting louder, broke her reverie and an incongruous motor scooter appeared at the end of the street. It buzzed past her and vanished round the corner. The anachronistic sound died away as swiftly as it had come. But the spell was broken. Holda turned and trudged back to where she had left her car.

She followed the signs towards Ghent and soon found herself back on the motorway, driving eastwards in the direction of Germany.

I was last in Meerbusch when I was ten years old, thought Holda. I wonder whether I'll even recognise it. I recollect the house where we lived and Schloss Pesch nearby, and the chapel, and a strange dark tower at the back that was fenced off. I know there were vast woods just behind the schloss. Or maybe they won't seem so large now that I'm grown up. There always used to be a young, ginger forester about there. Pater used to call him "homo silvestris" (orang-utan) instead of "silvarum custos" (woodsman). It was a typical Pater joke.

She paused in her recollections for a moment. It had never really struck her before how odd it was that she had grown up speaking Latin with her parents.

But it wasn't just classical Latin, she thought. If it had been, we couldn't have talked about anything that wasn't old. Mater and Pater had invented words for modern things too. They complained about the house being under the flight path - the 'iter aëronauticum' we called it. My bicycle was a 'birota' and we washed our clothes in a 'machina linteorum lavatoria'. The Latin I learned had evolved to incorporate technology and electronics and even space travel.

She paused to consider the implications of this. It means, she thought, that I must speak a language that nobody else speaks. A language which was created solely for me. And now they're dead, I am the only person left in the world that speaks it. Of course there are other people who understand Latin but is there anyone else who can actually use it to talk about science and learning, or even ask whether the vacuum cleaner bag is full?

She drove on past Ghent and picked up the signs for Antwerp.

What a terrible way to bring up a child, she thought. I never even thought about it until now, because it was all I'd ever experienced. They raised me to follow in their footsteps as a classicist, to carry on their life's work. They worried that the classics weren't being taught in schools and that I might never learn Latin or Greek if they didn't teach me. But to make Latin my actual mother tongue – that was a step too far. They brought me up for the first years of my life speaking no other language. I was literally unable to communicate with other children or adults. If I hadn't gone to Kindergarten when I was five I might never have learned to speak German. If we hadn't moved to Cambridge when I was ten, I might never have spoken more than basic school English with a German accent. She grimaced. Or an ancient Roman one, she added to herself wryly.

She drove on. Her mind was reeling at the implications of this chain of thought.

As a young child I was totally isolated from the community I lived in, she realized with bitterness. This is why I never learned to socialise. I was always alone, literally unable to communicate, not equipped to play with other children, and denied the same books or culture as them. I was only ever in the stifling hothouse of Pater and Mater's academic world. There were no siblings, uncles, aunts or grandparents. I only experienced whatever Pater and Mater gave me access to. I couldn't even understand television until I was already at primary school and had learned enough German. No wonder the other children bullied me. I must have seemed so weird to them.

By now the car was approaching Antwerp and the traffic was getting heavier. Holda decided against making another stop and joined the city ring road, watching keenly for signs to the Netherlands.

I must be the only Cambridge linguist who grew up unable to speak a modern language, she thought wryly.

Perhaps that's why I was drawn to medieval rather than modern German. Maybe I needed to go back in time and start learning the language right from the beginning. Could it be that I'm not ready for the modern world yet?

The sign for Eindhoven appeared and Holda turned gratefully off the congested Antwerp ring road onto a gloriously empty motorway.

Pater even gave me the nickname 'Adversaria' when I was little. It means blank jotter in their Latin. That must have been how he saw me. A set of unwritten pages for him and Mater to fill. I'm glad I rebelled against all that. That's why I chose German rather than classics and Holda rather than Aphrodite. Anyway, that's all over now. I must stop thinking about my parents on this trip. I told them they weren't coming with me. I need to be focussed on my own life and writing my own story from now on.

Holda jabbed her foot at the accelerator with a grimly determined look on her face and the car sped faster towards the Dutch border. But by the time she reached Eindhoven, Holda's resolution was already starting to waver.

It's all very well, she sighed inwardly, trying to write in my own adversaria but can I really steer the direction of my life? I can't even get the words together to plan my thesis. I've got writer's block in my academic research and it's spread to every other aspect of my life as well. I really hope this trip will help me overcome this sense of limbo.

As she crossed the border into Germany it was already getting dark and Holda was feeling dog-tired. Not long now, she told herself. Only half an hour more and I'll be at the hotel.

When she finally swung into the car park of the Hotel zur Krone in Meerbusch, the only thought in her mind was getting to bed. She ordered an alarm call for seven from the cheerful lady at the desk, instantly forgot all instructions about breakfast timings and parking arrangements, and took herself up one flight of stairs to a small but very clean room under the eaves. Within ten minutes she was drifting into a deep, dreamless sleep.

Chapter 3

It was ten to eight the next morning when Holda set out from the hotel. She had Azriel's note with Rupert Keller's address tucked firmly in her bag, along with a small leather pouch containing her precious manuscript kit. This consisted of two pairs of freshly laundered white cotton gloves, a tape measure, an antique ivory page turner and a powerful magnifying glass. She was dressed in her least shabby jeans and the pink trainers again, but this time she had teamed them with a pale blue shirt and oversized black cardigan.

It was only a short walk from the hotel up the Dorfstrasse to the town's administrative centre on the square. As the sun was shining, she chose to leave the car and go on foot. According to Azriel's note she had a meeting scheduled with the uncooperative Rupert Keller at eight.

That means he arranged the appointment before he even told me about the manuscript, she thought, and suddenly felt furious. Azriel knew I wouldn't refuse the mission. I'm just a puppet. He's pulling the strings on this episode in my life. I have to stop letting other people dictate what I do.

She crossed what the town's website describes as a square but which was more of an open air car park, and arrived at a long, squat, black and white building whose windows reminded her of hooded eyes. Inside, a lady in the reception room gave her directions up the stairs to the first floor. She quickly found the door with Rupert Keller's name and the word Stadtarchiv on it, and knocked timidly. A voice answered and she popped her head round the door.

Holda's initial impression was that she had definitely come to the wrong place. The room was light and furnished with the sort of cheap white furniture which always comes flat-packed. There were several filing cabinets and a shelf filled with grey ring binders. There was nothing whatever to suggest an archive or a library. Instead of a grumpy, elderly archivist there was a cheery, energetic young man in his late twenties rising from a swivel office chair and extending a hand with a broad smile. He was of medium height and slim build, with mousy blonde hair and the bluest eyes Holda had ever seen in her life. He wore jeans, a neat dark blue shirt and brown suede loafers.

"Holda Weisel?" he enquired in heavily accented English. "I am Rupert Keller. I spoke with Professor Finster last week and also yesterday about the arrangements for you to see the manuscript. Welcome to Meerbusch. Can I offer you a coffee?"

Holda introduced herself in German with what she hoped was a bright smile and gratefully accepted his offer of coffee. While he left the room to fetch the drinks, she tried to rally her thoughts.

I must focus on getting access to the manuscript and somewhere to work on it, she told herself sternly. He has the most beautiful eyes in the world and they crease up at the edges when he smiles, the innermost part of her brain answered.

Rupert Keller of the bright blue eyes returned with two steaming mugs of coffee, still beaming his welcoming smile. This time he spoke to her in German.

"Let me introduce myself and the town archive first," he proposed, "Then we can drive over and see the manuscript and you can tell me what you make of it."

Holda glanced at him quizzically. "Is the manuscript not kept here?"

"No, we've stored it in the old mill in Lank-Latum for now. You know Meerbusch is a community created out of eight separate villages, right? Büderich, Strümp, Lank Latum, Ossum and so on. We're in Meerbusch-Büderich right now, but the old Teloy windmill is about seven kilometres from here in a village called Lank-Latum. I put it in a cast-iron safe which we have there in an upstairs room."

Holda glanced at Keller sharply. "What kind of an archive do you have here?" she asked, genuinely suspicious now. The man obviously had no clue about the proper storage of old documents. He appeared to be pleasant enough so far, but she remembered Azriel's description of him and decided she ought to resist his charming gaze.

Keller sipped his coffee and smiled sheepishly. Despite herself, Holda felt her own mouth twisting up at the corners in a surprise response.

"The thing is," he explained, "although I studied to be a librarian and archivist, Meerbusch lost nearly all of its records in the second world war. In 1942 the village authorities here were ordered to pack up all the important documents and registers locally and deliver them to the nearby town of Neuss, from where they would be sent off somewhere for safe keeping. By the end of the war our town hall and municipal buildings were in ruins, except this one. In the mid-fifties a small number of archive boxes were returned to us from Neuss, but it was only a fraction of what we'd had previously. The rest were lost and nobody had any records of where they'd gone, or even what was sent away." Keller gave a wry smile. "It still causes problems to this day. Imagine a country like Germany where everything depends on you having all your documentation in order, and then suddenly the entire land registry, title deeds for buildings, birth, marriage and death records - everything more or less - is missing. Nobody could prove they owned their own house, that it was built legally, or that they'd inherited it legally and were entitled to sell it or leave it to their own heirs. For Germans it was a complete nightmare."

He took another sip of coffee. His gaze fell on her and she found herself staring again at those sapphire eyes. I wonder why Azriel thought he was so obnoxious, she wondered.

"So I am trying to build a new type of archive for Meerbusch," he continued. "I am the official collector of photographs, stories, letters and memories. I track down the older inhabitants and ask them about everything they remember. I go through their family photograph albums with them. I ask them about what they know of the history of old buildings; who lived there, what they did for a living. I collect details of how people farmed, travelled, what jobs they did, what tools they used, what they ate, what they wore. I record the interviews on audio or video and archive their stories. I collect the memories of those who built the schools here after the war, of those who were taught in those classrooms when they first opened. Not just the old folk either; I even interview today's kids about their Playstations and mobile phones. Those things may not sound interesting now, but in fifty years people will want to hear those accounts." Rupert Keller's face glowed with passion as he spoke.

He's a collector of stories, thought Holda. I was born in Meerbusch too but I don't have a story to tell him, because my story isn't my own. I've never really been writing it. It was always set down for me, first by my parents and now by Azriel. What would my own narrative even be? When will I start filling out the pages of my own blank book?

"It must be a fascinating archive," she encouraged him. "You must have gathered the memories of people who lived through interesting and turbulent times. The war stories especially must be riveting."

"Oh yes. We have first-hand accounts of what it was like during bombing raids, stories about hiking and camping with the Hitler Youth. We even have reports about when the first American tanks rolled through Meerbusch at the end of the war, about Americans being billeted with local families and handing out chocolate and chewing gum."

The usual sanitized version of the war, thought Holda to herself. It is the war that Meerbusch can live comfortably with. There will be no confessions of war crimes by local SS officers or Nazi officials, no recollections of Meerbusch citizens doing their military service as concentration camp guards. There won't be any first-hand accounts of the day a baying mob of villagers drove Jews from their homes and then looted their possessions. Nobody will point to a fine Meissen figurine on the sideboard and boast that their father stole that from a Jew. No-one will describe how satisfying it was to smash their neighbour's windows. There will be no anecdotes about forcing children onto cattle trucks at gunpoint and sending them east to die. No post-war soul searching will come to light. It will all be hiking and camping and being the helpless victims of bombing raids, followed by chocolate and chewing gum when it was all over.

"How wonderful," she responded instead. "It must be an interesting job."

"The newly found manuscript isn't the first discovery we have made," went on Keller. "Only seven years ago when we were renovating this very building, we found a fresco painted on the wall in the entrance hall. It had been plastered over and hidden for decades. This building was opened in 1939 you know, as the headquarters of the local Hitler Youth. It was called the Hermann-Göring-Heim back then and the Dorfstrasse was the Adolf-Hitler-Strasse. The mural dates back to that time. It is a massive stylised map of Meerbusch depicting the town as a Nazi idyll with hunting, agriculture, factories and happy Aryan yokels in traditional costumes."

"I didn't see that when I came in," exclaimed Holda in surprise.

"No," explained Keller. "We erected plasterboard in front of it and hung an aerial photograph of the town on the wall. It's preserved for posterity of course, but it's not socially or politically acceptable nowadays to display images of Nazi ideology in public, particularly not in the town hall. You can look at a photograph if you are interested, but we don't have it on show."

I wonder whether Johannes von Deibel's manuscript will pass muster, wondered Holda. Will it ever be allowed to be viewed by the public, or will it stay hidden in its cast-iron strongbox if it doesn't fit the sanitised official narrative? She drained her coffee cup and smiled encouragingly at Keller, her eyebrows raised.

"What can you tell me about this new discovery, Herr Keller?" she asked.

"Let's drive over there together and I'll tell you what I know on the way," Keller smiled back. "By the way, you can call me Rupert."

"And you can call me Holda," replied Holda grasping his outstretched hand and shaking it. She was familiar with the customs which Germans perform when they transition from formal to informal pronouns. A handshake, a request to be called by your first name and after that they would remain on 'du' terms for life.

Rupert retrieved a dark brown leather jacket from behind the door, pulled it on and then led the way downstairs and out into the main car park. His car was an ancient, and rather battered, black Ford. He shifted a pile of papers and some electronic equipment from the passenger seat to the rear.

"I'm scheduled to interview an elderly lady later today," he explained. "She grew up in the house next door to the old dairy building. I'm hoping to find out more about how the dairy used to operate in the 1930s when the milk was delivered by horse and cart. I always try to keep my recording gear in the car in case I meet someone with an interesting story to tell."

As they set off on the road towards Lank-Latum, Rupert began.

"The manuscript came to light because workmen are currently renovating the derelict chapel of Schloss Pesch up in Strümp – that's another of the Meerbusch communities."

"I know," replied Holda quietly, then bit her lip. She didn't feel ready to reveal her own story yet.

"They found a box bricked up inside the chapel wall and inside it was a leather bound book. The owner of the chapel didn't want to keep it and he brought it down to the town hall and donated it to us for the archives. It's handwritten, partly in Latin and partly in an old form of German, and looks ancient. It's definitely older than the schloss or its chapel which only date from the beginning of the nineteenth century. That's as much as I can tell you."

He paused, then added.

"There's something odd about the book though. When it was first given to us, I had it in my office in Büderich but it was making me feel..." He paused again. "Unwell," he came out with at last. "Or...out of sorts." His cobalt eyes flashed a quick, almost furtive glance at Holda.

"So I decided to store it in the safe in the Teloy wind-mill over in the village of Lank-Latum. That's another building owned by the town authorities. Teloy was the name of the miller whose family operated it for five generations. I've been fine again since it was kept there. It's probably a coincidence. It's likely I just had some flu virus running through me at the time. But I thought I'd mention it, just in case it affects you in any strange way."

"Thanks," replied Holda. In her mind she was running through a list of medieval illnesses: leprosy, bubonic plague, smallpox, anthrax. I hope it's not actually contaminated with something, she thought anxiously. But no, if it were anything like that, Rupert would not have recovered so quickly.

"Do you know how Professor Finster got to hear about its discovery?" she asked.

"That was due to our Bürgermeisterin, our lady mayor," answered Rupert with a wry grimace. "I believe Professor Finster is her husband's cousin or something of the sort, so she asked his advice about it when it first arrived. He insisted on sending you over post-haste and extracted a promise that we wouldn't let anyone else look at it until you'd had chance to evaluate it. He was quite rude on the phone actually. I should warn you: we won't let it out of our possession whatever happens. We have so few original documents that even if it turns out to be something dull, we're still grateful to have it.

The Teloy windmill turned out to be a picturesque, circular, brick-built construction in the classic Dutch style, with red sails and a rounded slate roof. The tower of the mill itself was perched on top of a wider circular building. On the ground floor inside was a tall round room directly under the mill, with other rooms leading off it.

"This central circular room on the ground floor is used for official functions," explained Rupert. "The washrooms are straight ahead and there's a kitchen on the left side. I can't guarantee there's any milk for tea or coffee, but you can get a glass of water at any rate."

A wooden staircase rose up from the main room, spiralling around the interior of the wall and leading to the partially exposed grinding mechanism and an upper floor room. It was up these steps that Rupert led the way.

In a room with exposed beams under the grey slates of the roof, lit by four small arched windows at the different points of the compass, he showed Holda a small cast-iron safe. Rupert turned a dial on the front until there was a distinct click, then swung open the door. He reached inside and withdrew a heavy blackened volume which he carried to a small table at one of the windows. He seemed to recoil slightly as he put it down.

Holda watched his every move intently and waited until he had withdrawn to the furthest side of the room. Then she fished into her bag and pulled out her mobile phone and her manuscript kit. Carefully she pulled on a pair of white cotton gloves, then turned on the recording device on her phone and began to speak into it.

"First viewing of the Johannes von Deibel manuscript in Meerbusch Lank-Latum at the Teloy windmill, May 16th at eight forty-five. The manuscript is a book fully bound in very dark or black leather. No visible inscription on the external boards but pronounced hubs from the binding cords on the spine, which are worn with use, as are the hinges and corners. Otherwise the binding appears tight and in good condition. Dimensions of the book are…" Holda put down the phone on the desk while she wielded her tape measure, then resumed. "Twenty-three centimetres height, seventeen centimetres width, just under three centimetres thick. No apparent signs on the exterior of any damp, mould or other damage."

Holda opened the cover.

"Front endpapers made from some recycled parchment, possibly formerly a roughly jotted tradesman's list. It includes items like candles and leather straps. Inscription on first leaf…" she paused. For a second her heart leapt to her throat.

"Inscription on the first leaf in medieval Latin – as far as I can make out: 'Investigationibus scientificis scripsit diarium quod Ioannes diaboli ab anno MCCCLXI.' That translates as: 'scientific research and diary written by Johannes the Devil in the year 1361'."

She clicked off the recording program and took a deep breath. You were right, Azriel, she thought to herself. Then remembering that Rupert was in the room, she turned round to see his response to her revelation. He was staring at her with a very strange, almost hostile expression on his face. With his back to the window opposite she could no longer see the colour of his eyes and the shadows on his face gave him an uncanny, almost malevolent aspect.

"Are you alright?" she asked nervously.

Rupert stepped towards her, forcing his face into a smile.

"I think I'll leave you alone here to study the manuscript," he announced with a laugh that didn't sound cheerful in the slightest. "I'll go round now and visit my old dairy lady. I'll come back and pick you up at lunchtime and we can go out for a pizza." He paused awkwardly and then added in a strangled tone, "I can't explain it, but that book gives me the creeps."

Before Holda could even reply, he had left the room with indecent haste.

As soon as he had gone, Holda peeled off her cotton gloves. She had worn them as a courtesy to Rupert, to indicate that she would take extreme care with his precious book. But clean hands are no worse for the manuscript than gloved ones, she thought. Anyway, it's much easier to turn the pages without damaging them if I use bare fingers.

Returning to the document she turned on her voice recorder again and began to speak.

"Pages are parchment, handwritten in what was probably black ink made from oak apples, now faded to near sepia. There is no table of contents. The first page contains what looks like a recipe in Latin for some sort of herbal cure." She pulled out her mother of pearl page turner and leafed through a few pages.

"More recipes. One of them is a sleeping draught. Another is a love potion for use on reluctant young girls." Holda smiled in amusement, then thought, I must go about this systematically. First I'll make an assessment of the whole book, then, while Rupert's not here to object, I'll photograph the pages so I can work on them in the hotel in the evenings. That way, if he does decide not to co-operate I've got images of all the text. I won't start actually reading it until I've worked out what's in the entire book. She leafed forward through some more pages then turned on her voice recorder again.

"It seems like there is more than one document bound together into a single volume. The herbal recipes stop after thirty-two pages, then there's a similar sized section on astronomy and the paths of the planets, also written in Latin," she dictated into her phone.

"After the astronomy part we get to von Deibel's diary. The entries are not dated. This part is written in Middle High German. Legibility might be an issue in some parts. This section seems to have been written much less carefully than the Latin parts, though the handwriting is similar. At least it's the same size and style. I'd say it was probably all written by the same person but in the early passages he may have been carefully copying from other documents. He was certainly paying more attention to making it legible. In the diary piece he's writing quickly and not worrying overmuch about neatness."

Holda turned over more of the stiff pages, counting the number of leaves under her breath.

"The diary part covers sixty-four pages. Then, at the end of the book, there's a set of blank pages which are made of a different material altogether. It's a light brownish colour and quite supple. I'd say it could be vellum. There's nothing written on either recto or verso leaves. There are eight of these blank leaves, so sixteen sides."

As Holda turned the last of the vellum pages she felt an involuntary shudder creep up her spine to the nape of her neck. Instinctively she looked around her but the room was empty. She went to the door and looked down the staircase, but there was nobody visible in the hollow chamber of the old mill.

It's that stupid thing Rupert said that's made me jumpy, she thought. There's nobody here.

She returned to the desk and switched the phone's function to camera. Then, starting with a shot of the closed book, she began to photograph each of the pages in turn, checking every picture to ensure that it was properly in focus and the characters legible. It took quite some time until she had reached the start of the blank section.

I'll take a picture of the first of the blank pages, just so I can show Azriel what it looks like, she thought, but I don't need photographs of sixteen plain sides.

She focused the phone camera and clicked. Then, as she looked back at the page, a frown passed over her features. She picked up her magnifying glass and examined the top of the page thoroughly. Then she checked over the picture she had just taken, blowing up it up and looking at the image minutely.

Just my imagination, she told herself, or a trick of the light. But how very odd the human brain is. I could have sworn I saw writing on the page just then and written in a quite different hand to the rest of the book. She grimaced to herself. It looked like the words 'Kom mich ze helf.' That's 'come and help me' in Middle High German. I wonder what put that into my head just then. Holda felt a tremor run through her. She closed the book carefully and took a deep breath. An over-active imagination is great for passing the time on car journeys, she observed to herself irritably, but not for other times. I wish Rupert hadn't told me about feeling unwell around the book. Now I'm feeling nauseous and shivery too. I wonder whether the windows here can be opened.

Holda grasped the brass window catch and found it swung back easily on well-oiled hinges. She gulped in the fresh air. At that very moment she heard footsteps on the stairs directly outside the room and swung round with a squeal of fright. Rupert stuck his head round the door. His face was now relaxed and cheerful.

"Are you ready for lunch?" he asked. "Sorry, did I give you a shock? I've just had a great interview with the milk lady. I learned a lot about butter churns and horse carts. How are you getting on with the old book?"

Holda shook herself and forced her mouth into what she hoped was a bright smile. "Fine," she answered, her voice a tone higher than usual.

"Just put the old volume back into the safe, close it and turn the dial on the front," added Rupert casually from the top of the stairs. He seemed in no hurry to enter the room.

Holda did as he asked. The volume felt warm and heavy to the touch. There must have been a vein pulsing in her middle fingertip as it really seemed to Holda, as she placed it in the safe, that the book was ever so slightly throbbing. With another involuntary shiver she slammed the door and span the dial on the front.

"Let's go," she urged curtly, even though her appetite had suddenly faded.

Chapter 4

Lank-Latum turned out to have a pretty cobbled pedestrian area with a fountain, and several cafés with outdoor seating. Half-timbered buildings surrounded them and a solid looking church squatted at one edge of the main square. The pair ordered a sparking apple juice each and shared a pizza margherita.

Rupert regaled Holda with anecdotes of his morning's recording of the old lady who had grown up around the village dairy, most of which seemed to involve spillage of vast quantities of cream. Holda quickly recovered from her earlier queasiness and found herself laughing out loud. It was a strange feeling hearing her own voice making such an unfamiliar sound. Then, as they were finishing the pizza, Rupert suggested, "How about we take a spin up to Schloss Pesch so I can show you where the manuscript was found?"

Holda started. She was about to explain that she already knew Schloss Pesch but then felt embarrassed and awkward, as though this was a piece of information she really should have volunteered much earlier in their acquaintance.

"Thank you. That would be lovely," she replied shyly with what she hoped was a grateful smile and thought, not for the first time that day, how alluring those blue eyes were.

Holda insisted on paying for their lunch using some of Azriel's money. Then they returned to

Rupert's car and he swung its nose in the direction of Strümp.

"Of course, technically the schloss is not open to the public," explained Rupert. "It was converted into private apartments over twenty years ago. As a member of the town's authorities I am allowed into the grounds of course, so long as I'm on official business." He winked one eye and grinned. "Besides, nobody will stop us because everyone who lives there will assume we've come to see one of the other residents."

Nobody ever stopped me back then either, thought Holda. I used to come in over the way from the woods at the rear. There's a little path from the forest which leads over a field where the remains of a ruined building are, then past a pond with bulrushes and irises and along the fence up to Rapunzel's tower. The schloss and the chapel are just a little way beyond there. I could still find my way blindfolded. I never drove in at the front though.

"Where exactly was the book hidden?" she asked.

"It was bricked up in a niche in the wall just behind where the altar of the chapel would have been," replied Rupert. "It was encased in a box made of lead. It was seized shut and the workmen had to break it open. It wasn't too difficult as lead is quite soft. There was nothing else in the box apart from the manuscript. It was well protected and dry as you saw, even though the chapel itself was derelict and the roof leaked badly in several places. The eastern side was better preserved than the rest of the building. Here we are now. You'll see it for yourself in a moment."

Rupert swung the car off the main road and through an imposing set of square pillars which, if they had ever had them, had forfeited gates many decades ago. The driveway was lined with trees and had probably once been gravel, but repeated winters of Rhineland rain and snow had swamped the small stones in mud and now it was just a network of puddles and sludgy hollows. At the far end of the drive were some parked cars to one side, and a modern set of imposing ornamental gates.

Rupert parked next to the other cars then led the way to a side gate for pedestrians. Beyond it was a grandiose turning circle with a vibrant green lawn in the centre, and on the far side stood the schloss itself. It was a great yellow mausoleum of a building: four stories high with four square columns, a wide balcony over the grand entrance and further massive portals on the wings to right and left. The grey slate roof was studded with two rows of white dormer windows and there were skylights above them. Chimneys bristled from various points of the roof and right in the centre was a curious oval roof terrace with an ornamental iron balustrade. To the right was a large, red brick farm building with a barn, stables and other outhouses. To the left was a darker, two storied, yellow building with a clock tower on the roof and white wooden shutters flanking the windows. Beyond that, the circular domed chapel built of red brick and grey slate. The building was still surrounded by scaffolding and a couple of men in overalls were working on the roof.

It's completely familiar and yet utterly different to how I remember it, thought Holda. The grounds look well kept up now. The façade has been plastered and painted. Everything seems lived in. Back then it was like a haunted house with loose shutters slapping against scabby plaster and the grounds all overgrown with vicious nettles and rank brambles. She glanced down at her pink trainers. "I should have dressed up to come here," she grimaced.

Rupert smiled encouragingly at her. "You're fine exactly as you are," he reassured her. "The inhabitants aren't as aristocratic as they pretend to be, trust me."

The pair made their way clockwise around the turning circle and stood in front of the chapel. The brickwork had been newly pointed, the roof was being completely renewed and the mix of circular and tall arched windows looked modern, double glazed and snugly fitted despite being tailored to historical openings. A modern glass portico was being added onto the front of the building to allow light to flood into the domed interior. The doors were not yet fitted and the interior was unplastered. The age-ripened brickwork was visible throughout.

It's barely recognisable, thought Holda. It's going to be an amazing designer apartment for somebody. It's not my secret witches' lair any more though. Back then it had a big wire fence around it and signs to keep out. There was a loose part where you could squeeze through though, at least if you were a skinny child. It wasn't hard to get into the chapel itself as the door was rotten and hanging off its hinges.

"What do you know about the history of this place?" she asked Rupert.

"Well, there's been some kind of mansion around here since at least the early 14th century," he replied. "But it wasn't anything like what you see now. The original fortress burned down in 1583 during the Cologne wars between Catholics and Protestants. We don't know exactly where that house was situated. Another castle of the same name was rebuilt on the fields at the back of the park by the forest. That's about a hundred metres behind here. That schloss was burned down in 1795 during the Franco-Prussian war. The new manor house you see here was constructed between 1804 and 1808 to replace it. The two side wings were added even later, between 1906 and 1912 by the von Amberg family, so it's really relatively modern. Certainly the manuscript was in existence for centuries before it could have been hidden in the chapel here."

"Who built the chapel?" asked Holda.

"It was a lady called Henrietta von Hüls. She only lived here for a short time though. She died in 1808. It's a strange and rather horrible story. I'll tell you about it later though. Let's take a look inside the chapel first."

Rupert called up to the roofers to ask permission to enter the building site. The two men in overalls were happy to use the opportunity to climb down and pour themselves coffee from a thermos flask they had stored inside their van.

Rupert led the way into the chapel and went straight over to a square niche in the rough brickwork to the right of the entrance.

"This is where the lead box with the book was hidden," he explained. "The altar used to be just here in front of it. The niche may have been originally intended as a place to store the host, but it was bricked up to conceal its secret contents. The only reason the builders even found it was that the bricks used to cover the hole were thin and of poor quality, so they were crumbling badly and needed replacing. It's quite dry though."

He reached his hand into the niche and then withdrew it sharply with a shiver. He glanced at Holda sideways with narrowed eyes. "These old walls do stay weirdly cold," he commented uneasily.

"What are those marks over the niche?" asked Holda, pointing. Above the hollow were a series of scratches which looked like parallel wavy lines. To the left of the niche was a deeply scratched scribble, almost like a child's drawing of a ball of wool. To the right was something that looked like a noughts and crosses board.

"I've no idea," replied Rupert. "I'd never noticed them before."

They're witch marks, thought Holda. They're what people used to draw around their windows and fireplaces in the old days to stop evil getting in. But in this case, it's likely they're trying to stop evil from getting out. They're meant to keep Johannes von Deibel's thoughts safely bricked up in this niche. And now we've let the manuscript out.

Holda stretched her hand towards the niche. There was indeed a marked drop in temperature in that part of the wall. She felt above and below the niche.

"That's odd," she remarked. "The rest of the brickwork is just normally cold, but the niche is so icy that it almost hurts your hand." She suddenly felt a strange churning in the pit of her stomach and turned quickly to leave.

"Let's get out into the sunshine," she pleaded apprehensively as she realised that the seething in her stomach was a sensation of fright. "I feel a bit odd in here. It's probably the stale air," she added with a nervous laugh in a hopeless bid to sound relaxed.

Once outside in the sunshine again, Rupert led her around the back of the schloss. There was a large terrace with a stone balustrade overlooking a sweeping park surrounded by trees and with two lakes, one on either side of the lawn lower down.

It's so well kept now, thought Holda. It used to be an absolute jungle. I always felt drawn to this place. The wild gardens were the exciting part for a child. All the buildings had an uncanny atmosphere as though they might be haunted.

"Let's see if we can find the ruins of the previous house," she suggested and set off left to the familiar path down past Rapunzel's tower.

"I think it's this way," called Rupert, pointing to the right.

"No, we can get there this way," Holda corrected him, then realised again that she had not confessed yet that she knew her way around.

Rapunzel's tower, Holda realised with a shock when they reached it, was actually an ornamental brick folly built to disguise where the telephone wires entered the estate from the overhead network and were fed underground to the schloss itself.

I never realised that it had a purpose before, mused Holda. It was just a padlocked tower in the middle of the wood. I always assumed it was to imprison someone and keep them hidden from the world, rather than to connect the people here to the rest of humanity.

"What an absurd extravagance that is," commented Rupert. "Typical of the von Ambergs from everything I've heard. They had far more money than sense, at least in the period up to the first world war. They were the first people in North Rhine-Westphalia to have a motor car you know. They had it decorated with their coat of arms on the doors as though it were a state carriage. There's a heliographic engraving of it in the Krefeld archives. We only have a photograph of it. What wouldn't we give to get hold of the original, but they won't even loan it to us for an exhibition."

I wonder what it actually feels like to be an archivist without an archive, thought Holda. He's obviously doing his best to create a history for the town, but everything seems based on people's memories and subjective judgements. How can he justify saying the von Ambergs had more money than sense, just because they had a car and a decorated telephone exchange? I wonder what the terrible story of Henrietta von Hüls will turn out to be and how much of that will be based on hearsay and prejudice.

Then she thought, but is that much different from what I'm doing? Will Johannes von Deibel's diary just be his subjective thoughts, or did he record factual happenings from his time? And why were there witch marks around the niche - what was he writing about? Holda felt in a sudden urgent hurry to get back to her hotel room to upload her photographs of the manuscript.

They walked onward, following the path down past the reedy lake to a rusty old kissing gate. Beyond it was a field with a handful of cows grazing among a network of old stone ruins forming a huge rectangular shape in the rough grass. Behind that the forest rose up darkly. No part of the remaining walls was more than a metre high. Holda recognised them immediately as the remains of the burned down schloss, although any charring or soot had long been washed away by centuries of Rhineland inclemency.

I used to jump off the ruins into the long grass, she thought. There were cows here then sometimes too. You had to watch out for cowpats when you jumped. And you had to watch for homo silvestris, the orang-utan. He'd be watching you from the woods. You could feel him there, even if you couldn't see him. That's why I hated 'The Jungle Book' film at kindergarten which they showed on rainy indoor days. The monkeys were too scary, jumping around the ruins and kidnapping human children.

"Tell me about Henrietta von Hüls?" she asked. "What was so horrible about her story?"

Rupert walked a little way into the fields, towards the tumbled down walls of the ruined house, and sat down on the low edge of the old foundations.

"Henrietta inherited the old schloss. She seems to have been a strange woman. In those days she'd have been quite the catch for any suitor of course, with her title, castle and lands. Apparently she was also thought to be quite a beauty, although no portraits of her have survived and you do have to take those kind of reports with a pinch of salt when they're spoken of the rich and powerful. The main reason I give no credence to reports of her beauty though is that, despite being the most marriageable female in the region, she seemed to have repelled all suitors right up to her death when she was in her forties."

"That's the privilege of having control of your own money," said Holda. "Most young women were married off by their parents in those days, without much say in the matter."

"Well, for whatever reason, Henrietta managed to avoid marrying," continued Rupert. "She had a reputation for being arrogant and vindictive. There was also some scandalous gossip linking her to a Dutch academic who she spent a lot of time with; a man from the University of Utrecht who first came here in 1789 with Alexander von Humboldt. He was apparently a botanist and was busy mapping the flora and geology of the Rhine region. He was a regular visitor apparently and he is said to have died in the fire here in 1795, along with a groom and two housemaids."

"What caused the fire?" asked Holda, seating herself on the wall a couple of metres away and instinctively glancing over her shoulder at the forest behind her.

"We don't really know," answered Rupert. "It was the time of the Franco-Prussian war and there were French troops in this area, but there is no record of any military incident here at that time. If there was any information it may have been in the part of the town archives that was lost. But after the fire Henrietta had the house rebuilt in grand style, as you see back there. Then, four years later, she was found murdered in very strange circumstances in the chapel of the schloss."

Holda started to her feet.

"The chapel where we just were?" she gasped, wide-eyed.

The chapel where I used to play as a child, she thought. No wonder I always felt scared of it. I could almost sense something horrible had happened there. She slumped down onto her rough stone seat again after another swift scan of the dark trees behind her.

"That's right. One morning she was found to be missing from her apartments. A search was made and eventually her naked, decapitated body was discovered spread-eagled on the altar between a pair of chantry candles, which were still lit but almost burnt down. Her right hand had been cut off and her tongue gouged out. Allegedly they found strange devilish markings drawn in pitch on the floor and also daubed on the dead body. Her hand was never found and neither was her tongue. Nothing else was taken, not even the chapel silver. On the floor behind the altar there was lying another body, that of an older man in his fifties or sixties. His head had been smashed in with a rock. He was so badly disfigured that it was not possible to identify him for certain. He was certainly not part of the household, though some people claimed he bore a resemblance to the Dutch academic who had been burned to death when the old house went up in flames. The morning when they found the bodies, a yeomen who used to run the farm, a man by the name of Heinrich Plenkers, was also found to be missing along with one of the horses. Everyone agreed Plenkers was not the dead body in the chapel. He was much younger and of far more athletic build than the corpse. Plenkers was sought for years afterwards on suspicion of the murders, but nobody ever saw him again. Henrietta and the unknown man were buried separately in Ossum. The chapel was deconsecrated and locked up, which is why it went to rack and ruin. After that, as Henrietta had no heirs, the house passed into the hands of the Geir family and from them by marriage to the von Ambergs."

"Was the manuscript hidden in the chapel before or after the murders?" queried Holda. "I wonder whether the two incidents are related."

Rupert glanced across at her quizzically. He looked as though he was going to ask her a question but then stopped. A strange, irritated expression flitted across his features for a moment.

"I don't know enough about the manuscript yet," she snapped in response to his unspoken inquiry. "I haven't had chance to read it. I'll need a couple of days at least to get a good overview of its contents. Let's go back, it's getting chilly."

With a shiver she rose and the two of them retraced their steps through the park, past the chapel and the schloss, to where Rupert's car was waiting.

"Can I get access to the manuscript again tomorrow?" she asked.

"Call round at my office at nine. I'll take you up there again," answered Rupert, but his voice already betrayed unease.

Chapter 5

After Rupert dropped her off at the Hotel zur Krone, Holda went straight to her room, fired up her laptop and uploaded the images from her camera. She scrolled past the earlier sections until she reached the first of the scrawled pages in Middle High German. Then she increased the image size to fill the screen and began slowly to decipher the handwriting, jotting down a transcription and simultaneously translating it in a blank notebook as she went. Gradually the first entry began to unfold under her ballpoint pen:

These pages are the journal of the alchemist and necromancer Johannes whom the hateful monks of Kaiserswerth named Deibel after their enemy Satan. Their intention was to alienate me from all humanity. They used me cruelly as though they had indeed captured Satan and held him in their power. For this wrong, and for the cruel murder of my parent Quirinus, may lightning strike them when they shit in the latrines above the monastery cesspit!

Those accursed monks named me a devil. A fiend I have therefore become. Soon a greater beast than myself shall I induce to rise out of the pit of flame. I shall cause one to be brought forth from my own loins who will wreak death and bitter destruction on all the world, until mankind cowers before my name and that of my magnificent child, ruler of all Hell's demons.

My life began in wretchedness but I have used my time to gain knowledge. I have travelled to Siena, Bologna, Naples. I have consulted scholars from Oxford to Toulouse, from Murcia to Fes. I spent three years in Heidelberg and two in Cambridge. I have studied the old texts and lore. I have absorbed the properties of plants, beasts and reptiles, and the constellations of the planets. I have learned the wisdom of the ancients. Now, for the past ten years, I have made my own research in my tower here on the Rhine and I am at the point of transilience.

Twelve days from now the planets will be aligned and all will be ready. I know the potions I will need. I have memorised the incantations and learned how to perform them. All the apostate symbols are now familiar to me. When I bring all these elements together under this planetary sequence, Lucifer himself will rise and may take possession of my humble body. At that moment a virgin vessel must be present awaiting his seed. Then he may, if he sees fit, through my loins, conceive a child which shall be the anti-Christ and will wreak Lord Satan's revenge on Earth, and on Saint Michael and his self-righteous angels.

I have selected an auspicious woman for this high office. She is Marieken, seventh daughter of the House of Pesch, here on the fertile side of the Rhine. She is newly returned from the convent at Düsseldorf. This virgin I shall procure in the days to come and keep her here in the tower until the moment arrives for my Lord and Master to impregnate her. I have twelve days in which to capture her. With my Master's help, it shall come to pass.

Holda pushed back her chair and stared at her own notes in alarm. Her heart was palpitating wildly. As her eyes darted back to the screen with the awful medieval text on it, she fought down rising panic. She made herself breathe slowly, counting each exhalation, and gradually she recovered her composure. Suddenly there was a ding and an alert in the corner of the screen showed her that an email from Azriel had arrived in her mailbox. Holda groaned inwardly. She slammed shut the jotter she had been transcribing into. Then she stretched out a finger to the track-pad of her laptop, slid the cursor past the medieval text to the bottom of the screen, and opened the email. Once Johannes von Deibel's words were no longer visible she felt calmer.

Dr. Finster's message was curt and to the point:

Holda, how is the manuscript? Send me your first assessment. Azriel.

The email helped Holda focus her thoughts and jolted her into action. Quickly she typed up a reply which was a summary of the comments she had made on her mobile phone's voice recorder that morning. Then she added: I'm starting to read the diary part next. It's in rather tricky handwriting. It may take me a while. I'll send a transcript as soon as I'm done.

She pressed send. She wasn't ready to share the entry she had just transcribed with Azriel yet. She didn't even want to look at it herself. She had to think, think...but her mind felt numb. Slowly she opened the notebook again and stared at the unfamiliar handwriting.

I didn't write that, screamed Holda in her head. That's not my writing and it's not von Deibel's script either. I don't form my letters like that. She looked at it again, this time in wide-eyed disbelief.

It's the handwriting I thought I saw on the blank page of the manuscript, she gasped to herself. I am actually going mad. The manuscript's making me delusional. Surely a book can't be cursed? What am I thinking? I can't start to believe in any of that nonsense.

All of a sudden she felt suffocated there in the hotel room. She grabbed her parka, purse and room key and ran downstairs and out of the hotel. The evening was still light and she set off up the Dorfstrasse, past the town hall, until she reached the station. On the other side of the tracks, she took a road to the left which crossed flat fields. It led her onward for a mile, past a couple of isolated farms and then, in the distance, she saw the dyke which runs along the Rhine rising up in the distance.

Once there she was able to look out over the huge, grey expanse of tree-lined river. A couple of giant barges were making their way lazily upstream with cargoes of containers and cars. She sat down on a bench and watched the scene below. The brisk walk had settled the worst of her panic. She needed time and space away from the manuscript so she could think. Up there the wind caught at her face and made it sting. The sun hung in the sky above a modern suspension bridge, downstream to her left. As she surveyed the scene the orb grew orange and descended slowly. The deep flowing water gradually transformed from slate grey to gold. Behind her on the dyke the only sounds were of late cyclists whizzing past anonymously, and once or twice dog walkers greeted her but without slowing their pace. Before long they too had disappeared.

In the stillness as dusk gathered, Holda began to muster her thoughts.

That manuscript is evil from start to finish, she decided. The man who wrote it was vile. The thoughts in it are evil. It was hidden in a place where a heinous crime was committed. There's a repulsive aura about it. It exerts a malevolent influence on the places and people around it. Rupert feels it and so do I. Even transcribing from a photo it somehow changes the way I write and how I feel. My handwriting looks like something from the fourteenth century. I'm terrified of my own notes. I feel completely out of my depth and yet I also don't want to tell any of this to Azriel. On the one hand it sounds crazy and on the other hand...her thought trailed off as she hesitated to complete the sentence that was forming in her head.

"On the other hand Azriel already knows about Johannes von Deibel and the manuscript is exactly what he was hoping it would be," she declared suddenly aloud to herself in Latin. It was still the language she used to form her innermost thoughts.

"Oh, excuse me, I didn't mean to startle you," an elderly man's voice spoke directly behind her, but in German. Holda span round in fright and found an elderly, rather tubby, friendly-looking gentleman in a black overcoat and broad brimmed hat standing smiling at her, just behind the bench.

"I was about to speak to you," the stranger went on. "I hope you don't mind, but a young woman like yourself sitting alone by the Rhine at nightfall...I just wanted to make sure you were alright. There have been cases..." His voice hesitated a moment before he continued. "I live in the house just over there where the river bends.

I spotted you from my window, sitting here by yourself on this bench. You'd be amazed how many people come and sit just here while they think about ending their lives in the river. It's probably because it's the first seat you get to when you've walked up from Büderich. It only takes me a moment to come up here and check on them. Just a few words, you know, is sometimes all it takes. I am a priest, retired now of course." He paused and looked at Holda with serious grey eyes. "Is there something troubling you?" he asked pointedly.

"No," stuttered Holda mechanically. Then, "Yes... oh, I don't know. It will sound so stupid and unbelievable if I try to tell you about it."

The old priest sat down on the bench beside her.

"Just try," he urged. "Sometimes just telling someone makes everything easier. Maybe I can help you, or maybe you will be able to help yourself. Is there anything to lose by trying?"

"I don't suppose so," answered Holda wretchedly. "It's not what you think anyway. I'm not suicidal. And I warn you, I'm not Catholic."

"We can sit here in the cold and dark to talk, if you like," answered the priest. "Or we can walk back the three hundred metres to my house, I can make you a hot drink and we can sit by the fire. What do you say?"

Holda smiled at him self-consciously in answer and got up. His unsolicited kindness had overwhelmed her and at that moment she didn't trust herself to speak.

As they set off along the dyke path, the priest introduced himself.

"I am Father Jacobi," he told her.

"Holda Weisel," answered Holda. "Please call me Holda, Father."

As she said it she realised with a start that she had never called anyone by that name before. She had never even spoken German or English with her own parents.

"Now tell me something," went on Father Jacobi. "When I reached you just now you were speaking to yourself in a language that sounded just like Latin. Yet you say you are not Catholic, and your German is perfect. Where are you from?"

Holda took a deep breath and for the rest of their walk she briefly explained the story of her isolated childhood and her academic career, ending with her journey to Meerbusch the day before. By that time they had arrived at a cluster of four or five ancient brick buildings, some of which looked agricultural. Jacobi unlocked the door of the largest, which was the only one with lights on. He guided Holda into a dim hall where he hung her parka and his own hat and coat on large iron pegs. Then he led the way into a snug living room where he proceeded to throw hunks of wood from a basket into a cast-iron log burner, on the top of which sat a domed steel kettle.

Soon Holda was cupping her hands around a steaming mug of tea and wondering how on earth to embark on the next part of her story. The kindly face on the other side of the stove smiled encouragingly but did not speak. The silence began to feel oppressive.

"Father, do you believe in Satan?" she asked at last.

"I believe there is great evil in the world," answered Jacobi cautiously. "Is that what you mean by Satan? Or do you mean a creature with cloven hooves and horns?" His eyes twinkled but his chubby face was earnest, attentive, subtly prompting her to keep telling her story.

"I don't even know what I do mean," answered Holda bitterly. "The book was written by an evil man. I've only read the first entry in his diary and it's talking about how he wants to summon the devil and kidnap and rape a virgin so she will bear a child who is the anti-Christ."

"That does indeed sound very wicked," reflected Jacobi. "I myself would not wish to read about such things, even though it was all written centuries ago and the man's soul must long ago have answered for these sentiments before his maker. Words in a book can do you no harm, child, so long as your heart remains steadfast against sin. But temptation can be very strong. The fact that you are troubled by what you have read shows that you are currently strong against such evil ideas. All the same, you must be vigilant. Tell me more about the book; it interests me."

"You don't understand, Father. I'm not so impressionable that I'd be seduced into devil worship by his writing. His words are vile, repulsive, they appal me... they are the work of a real demon. In fact the whole manuscript is horrible."

"You have free will, my dear, and you must use it wisely. That has always been mankind's greatest challenge. We have repeatedly to choose between right and wrong, good and evil. It is the nature of life that the choices are not made easy for us."

That may be true for other people, thought Holda. But I never had any free will. My life was always dictated by other people. I'm on a conveyor belt trundling towards some pre-ordained destiny and I don't know how to get off it.

The old priest sipped his tea and then continued.

"You asked me about Satan. I can tell you that there are many passages both in the Old and New Testaments which mention the devil, but the references are frequently obscure and hard to interpret. The main area of contention between the church and devil worshippers relates to the origin of Satan and his demons. Satanists claim that God created the entire universe, incorporating both Heaven and Hell, and that good and evil are therefore equally part of the divine plan. They portray God and Satan as well matched but polemic adversaries in a constant struggle for the souls of mortals. At the point of death, each will reject and cast out any soul which could not be won to their side during their lifetime."

"Forgive me, I wasn't brought up in a religious family," commented Holda cautiously, "but isn't that how the church sees it too?"

"It is one of the strangest aspects of the Bible," continued Jacobi, ignoring her interruption, "that for the only full account of the Fall of Angels, which preceded the creation of the world, we have to turn to the very last book of all, the Revelation of St. John. The Fall is described as a great war in Heaven between Michael and Lucifer, who is portrayed as a mighty dragon, and between their respective angel armies. Lucifer and his angels were cast out of Paradise and fell to Earth. The church's point is that Lucifer and his followers were created by God as good angels, but of their own free will they chose to become evil. Lucifer's crime was to desire independence from God and equality with God."

He looked at Holda gravely.

"So long as you resist the devil's temptations your soul will be destined for Heaven. As soon as you let the devil's words lead you from the right path, you are in mortal danger."

Holda looked across at the old priest's face, illuminated by the flicker of the burning logs. How kindly he looks, she thought to herself. Can someone who is godly really understand what I am trying to tell him?

"It's not the words, Father," she suddenly blurted out urgently, fiercely. "It's the book itself that's evil. Even if you haven't read it, it makes you feel afraid, angry, wicked. Rupert felt it too, the town archivist. He doesn't read Latin or medieval German but he couldn't keep it in the same room as himself. It makes terrible things happen. Just there, where it was hidden, there was a gruesome double murder over two hundred years ago. It's almost as though the book is..." she stopped, afraid of the word she had been about to use, but then she hissed it anyway, "possessed."

She took stock of the priest's facial expression as she spoke.

He doesn't believe me, she realized. He thinks I'm mad, or hysterical, or deluded. Perhaps I am all of those things. He's smiling as though it's a fairy tale I'm telling.

"Would it ease your mind," asked Jacobi in his kind, steady voice, "if I bestow a blessing on you for tonight and if I accompany you to the windmill tomorrow and bless your manuscript? It may be that some of the aura of its writer still hangs about it."

It can't do any harm, thought Holda. But will it do any good?

"I'll be at the Teloy windmill all morning," she announced in response.

The priest stood up and placed his hands on Holda's head, pronouncing, "De profundis clamavi ad te,

Domine. Domine, exaudi vocem meam et libera nos a malo."

Holda looked up in sudden fright. She had understood his words. They meant: out of the depths I have cried to thee, O Lord. Lord, hear my voice and deliver us from evil.

"Deliver me from evil?" she cried out in alarm.

"I think," replied Jacobi slowly, "that you may be in more danger than you realise. You are certainly being tested. Remember that whatever words you read in that manuscript, Satan is telling you lies. Salvation is not his to offer. All he can give you are sins, follies, disappointment, death and eternal damnation. His overtures can sound very alluring though. He will seek out your weaknesses and try to exploit them."

He gave Holda his hand and raised her to her feet.

"I will walk with you as far as the village," he reassured her. "We will resume this conversation tomorrow at the windmill. For now we will talk of other matters. You won't sleep well if your head is full of fearful thoughts."

As they walked back together towards the town, he diverted her with a long story about a friend whose donkey had recently escaped into a neighbour's kitchen. But even as Holda laughed aloud at the absurdity of the priest's tale, she sensed her unease growing as every step took her nearer to her notebook and the words of Johannes von Deibel.

Chapter 6

Holda was awake at seven the next morning, far too early to set off to meet Rupert. She went down for the hotel's breakfast, then returned to her room and flipped open the laptop to check for email. She had deliberately ignored it the night before on the advice of the old priest, who was insistent on keeping her thoughts diverted from her project during the hours of darkness. There was a message from Azriel from the previous evening:

Send transcription in sections as you go along. Do not wait. There is no time to lose. Also, keep an eye on the blank pages bound into the back of the book and report back anything unusual.

He knows much more than he's told me, thought Holda. It isn't fair of him not to share his knowledge. He's read things about this book from other medieval scholars and he's deliberately not briefed me. But then if he had, I'd have thought it was him putting ideas in my head, leading to that uncanny plea for help which I thought I read on the blank page. Maybe he really needed me not to know how that book works.

She shook her head as if to push away the thoughts and sat down to type up yesterday afternoon's transcription. She copied the text into an email to Azriel and clicked 'send'. Then, with a glance at the clock in the top corner of the screen, she closed down her laptop and stuffed it, along with her notebook and phone, into a shoulder bag and set out in the direction of Rupert's office. The sun was shining but there were many large clouds about, especially in the west. Some of them looked threatening.

That's the advantage of the flatlands, thought Holda. You can see the entire sky so the weather doesn't catch you unawares. The weather nearly always comes from the same direction, from the west and the sea. Everyone can see there's going to be a storm later on.

Rupert was in a cheerful mood. He had Holda's coffee freshly brewed for her and he had managed to produce half a packet of biscuits. For an instant she found herself involuntarily gazing at those glorious blue eyes of his before realizing she was at risk of making an idiot of herself. She blushed and quickly turned her attention to her drink.

"I might have something of interest for you," he reported. "I sent off a couple of email enquiries to the archives in Düsseldorf, Krefeld and Duisburg to see whether they have anything concurrent to the manu-script for the year 1361. Düsseldorf got back this morning to say they definitely have court records dating from that year. I've asked them to send through a scan of them. When it arrives and you want a break from ploughing through that horrible old book, I'll show it to you. It might be useful to you to know what else was going on locally at that period."

"Thank you, that's great," replied Holda. "Though I think it would make sense to wait until I've read the book first. Otherwise I won't know what I'm looking for."

"Suit yourself," he grinned cheerily. "I might pop over there next week and see what else they have. I want to put together an exhibition in the town library about the book, so I'll need plenty of background material. You can decide whether you're far enough through it to join me, or at least give me a few hints about what to look for. I want to work out what the Meerbusch villages would have been like back in 1361. None of the buildings from that time have survived. What would they have looked like? How would people have lived?"

A pint-sized version of the backstreets of Bruges, thought Holda, but built on river silt. The Meerbusch villages were rural farming communities. Stinking people lived in muddled clusters of dilapidated buildings teeming with noisy animals. The wealth was all with the few aristocrats and the church. Everyone else's life was a struggle. Disease and death were commonplace; more children died than survived their first year. I wonder whether the modern citizens are ready to get to know their own ancestors, let alone Johannes von Deibel.

"I can help you with all the background," she said, "but Rupert, I need to ask you something first. Have you heard of a Catholic priest called Father Jacobi?"

"Old Papa Jacobi?" answered Rupert, his smile vanishing and his lip curling to a grimace. "Of course I have. He was the priest here for nearly thirty years. I believe he still lives locally, though I haven't seen him for years, thank goodness. I was baptised by him. I sang in his choir until I was nine. I nearly flunked his confirmation classes. He used to be horribly strict with the choirboys. I hated him to be honest and was relieved when our family switched to a church in a different village. How do you know about him?"

So Rupert is Catholic too, she thought. That might make things easier.

"I met him yesterday evening," explained Holda. "I want to show him the manuscript today and I asked him to come over to the windmill this morning."

She hesitated. "He is going to say a prayer over the manuscript," she confessed awkwardly. "I mean, if that's OK with you."

"Jacobi at the windmill? To say a prayer?" Rupert's voice sounded incredulous. Then his face suffused with anger. "You mean he claims he's going to drive out some evil spirits from the book? Not if I have anything to do with it! Stay away from Jacobi, Holda. He's not a nice man. He's invited himself because he fancies you. Don't listen to his fake prayers. His blessing won't count for anything. Everything that man does has an ulterior motive."

Holda gaped at Rupert for a moment. I wonder why he's so hostile towards the old priest, she thought. Is the manuscript affecting him again after he came back into contact with it yesterday? Is that what it does - make people angry, suspicious, mistrusting?

"He thought his prayers might lay any bad influence of the manuscript to rest," she explained simply.

"So you felt that odd sensation around the manuscript too?" asked Rupert triumphantly, then his face clouded over again.

"But it's all rubbish of course. I only felt out of sorts because I was ill, or maybe the book is harbouring toxic mould spores or something. Seriously, we can't be seen to be calling in a priest. I don't want that man involved. I mean, what would everyone think? It would look so unprofessional and superstitious. I could lose my job."

"It's me who invited him, not you," snapped Holda sharply. "I want to ask his advice. Rupert, the whole manuscript is about Satanism and raising the devil. I don't know anything about those things. I need someone who understands the background theology."

I wonder why he is overreacting like this, thought Holda. Nobody will even find out about the priest's visit. That thing he claimed about the priest fancying me is absurd. The man is in his seventies. Rupert is obviously a lapsed Catholic and about as insufferable about it as an ardent ex-smoker is about smoking. I wonder if he has something on his conscience that he doesn't want Father Jacobi to know about. Or more likely he wants to avoid him because there's something embarrassing he's confessed to, that Father Jacobi does know about.

For a moment Rupert also seemed lost in grim thought. Then suddenly he gave an involuntary shudder and a lop-sided grin stretched across his face.

"An exhibition about Satan worship and witchcraft would definitely draw the crowds," he mused. "It wouldn't just be a local event either. They'd come from all over the region for that. We could be on to something big here. Come on, let's get over to the windmill."

As they arrived in Lank-Latum the dark clouds which Holda had noticed earlier were closer and blacker. Rupert squinted up at them as he locked the car.

"Looks like we're in for a storm," he observed. "Let's get indoors before it starts."

He unlocked the windmill door and led the way up the spiral staircase to the room at the top. He opened the safe door but this time let Holda bring the manuscript out and place it on the table by the window.

He still kept his distance from the manuscript, but his expression was now one of keen concentration.

How odd that the book feels so smooth and warm even though the room is not heated, thought Holda. It's almost like touching somebody's bare skin.

She shuddered and pulled on her cotton gloves, no longer as a courtesy to Rupert, but because she didn't want to make physical contact with those pages.

Rupert watched intently as she showed him the different sections of the manuscript.

"We could build a fabulous exhibition around this," breathed Rupert, almost to himself. "We could turn each of these herbal potions into its own exhibit. The astrology part we can illustrate with models. It's probably too early to say what we could do with the diary."

"You could try illustrating the curses," suggested Holda mischievously. "What were monastery latrines like in the 1360s and how could you best survive a lightning bolt while using one?"

A sound downstairs interrupted their ensuing laughter. Rupert stepped out onto the staircase and looked down.

"Oh, is that you, Papa Jacobi?" he called down. "Do you remember me - Rupert Keller? The boy who broke your vestry window with a catapult. I should have aimed at your head, Father." He laughed too loudly and his voice echoed, oddly mirthless, around the hollow mill. Then he added, "Holda and I are right up here in the rafters. Can you manage the climb?"

Holda couldn't catch the priest's reply but a couple of minutes later she heard laboured puffing and gasping outside, and a rather flushed pink face peered around the door.

"It's like climbing Jacob's ladder, getting up here," panted the portly priest. "You'll be telling me next that the only toilets are on the ground floor."

Rupert looked irritated rather than amused at the joke.

"You know quite well there is neither plumbing nor electricity up here, Papa," he retorted.

How rude Rupert is, thought Holda. I'm not religious but even I think you should treat the clergy with respect. He has forgotten his manners completely. I wonder whether he was this obnoxious to Azriel. That would explain why he called him uncooperative. Surely it can't really be the book that's making him like this?

"Good morning Holda, and hello Keller you young scoundrel," continued the priest. "So, I have been summoned from the other end of Meerbusch to cast out the devil from a book, only to find everyone enjoying a great joke. Not at my expense I trust?"

"Oh no, Father," exclaimed Holda, mortified. "We were laughing about monastery latrines."

"Ah well, whether that's humorous is a matter of opinion," countered the priest. "I spent a year once at a Jesuit school in Göttingen which had the most dreadful antediluvian plumbing. I could tell you no end of stories about those privies."

"Let me show you the manuscript I was telling you about last night," interrupted Holda hastily. With Rupert's rude irritability and her own pervasive unease, she was suddenly in no mood for anecdotes and banter.

She guided Father Jacobi to the table at the window and began to show him the book. She turned over the pages with gloved hands and pointed out the sections. When she got to the diary part she began to translate aloud the paragraphs about raising the devil and abducting a local girl. She hadn't got far into it though before she had to break off.

"It's so dark all of a sudden," she complained. "I can scarcely make out the sepia ink on the parchment. It must be the storm coming."

"From what I have heard so far, it is no bad thing if we don't read on," commented Jacobi. He was bending low over the book, peering at the writing. At that moment a silver crucifix which he had on a chain around his neck broke free from where it had been snagged on his lapel and swung down, its base brushing the parchment page in front of him. Simultaneously, a deafening rattle, like machine gun fire, broke out all around them. They stared at each other in bewilderment for a moment.

"It's hailstones," cried Rupert, with something like relief in his voice. "It's this loud because we're right up under the slate roof."

A glance out of the window confirmed his conclusion. There were hailstones the size of walnuts hurtling down from the sky.

"The tiles are breaking," screamed Holda suddenly. Then, "Oh my God! Oh my God!"

The room was suddenly so black she barely saw the window blow inwards, shattering glass over her, as a strut from the windmill sail hurtled through one pane.

"Everybody get out, get downstairs!" yelled Rupert.

Holda grabbed her bag and ran to the door. Rupert waited as Holda and then Father Jacobi passed through the doorway and onto the staircase, then he ducked back indoors and slammed the book into the safe, spinning the dial furiously before sprinting back to the exit.

As he ducked through the door, part of the roof fell down in a massive cloud of choking dust. A beam barely missed his head and a chunk of slate caught his shoulder and neck, causing his left arm to go limp. He gave a howl of pain but still managed to follow Holda and Jacobi down the wooden spiral steps at a fair speed. He repeatedly glanced backwards up the staircase and then downwards as he went, as though fearful that the whole staircase might give way beneath them all. Pieces of plaster and debris were raining down from above.

Half way down Rupert caught up with Father Jacobi, who had a gash to his forehead, and Holda, who was grey with dust and bleeding from several lacerations she had received from the shattering window. They all hurried as quickly as they could to the bottom of the tower and stood huddled together in fright under a solid brick arch, as masonry, broken timbers and hailstones clattered down in front of them.

Father Jacobi muttered something in Latin under his breath that sounded like a prayer, but Holda couldn't make out the words through the roaring above them.

It seemed like an age before the noise died down, the crashes giving way to rattles as only hailstones hit the tiled floor.

"What the holy fuck was that?" gasped Holda. Then, "Sorry, Father."

"Under the circumstances, I'll overlook it," responded Jacobi, pulling out a handkerchief and wiping blood and grime from his eyes. "Whatever it was though, it certainly wasn't holy."

Rupert peered upwards.

"The whole roof's gone," he cried out. "That was no ordinary storm." Then, looking round at the others,

"You're both bleeding and I think I may have broken my shoulder or something."

"We should stay here until the hailstones stop," cautioned Jacobi. "Some of them are like golf balls. We're safest where we are."

They stayed put. Holda felt herself shivering uncontrollably until Rupert put his good arm around her, which felt strangely comforting. Father Jacobi muttered something which Holda took for a quiet prayer and then embarked on a reminiscence of a great thunderstorm that had hit Meerbusch sometime in the 1950s. Neither Holda nor Rupert listened to the details, but the babble of his voice somehow served to take the edge off their agitation. Before he could finish, however, a noise at the entrance startled them and the mill's great door was pushed open. Two figures in fire-fighters' uniforms stepped cautiously through the portal. The dust was still thick in the air.

"Anyone here?" called one of them.

"Over here," shouted Father Jacobi.

"How many of you?"

"Three."

"Any injuries?"

"Yes. But not serious. Cuts and a possible fracture. We'll live. What happened?"

One fireman spoke into his radio and then came cautiously around the interior wall to where the three were standing.

"A tornado just blasted through this part of Lank-Latum," he announced. "It only lasted a few minutes but it's left a path of destruction. You were lucky you weren't up there when it hit." He pointed towards the roof. "The whole roof's off and the windmill sails are in splinters. Can you all walk? There's an ambulance on its way. You'll be safer outside. The rest of the roof beams might fall down any minute. Come on. Follow me."

He led them single file around the perimeter of the room and out of the doorway. They were greeted by blue flashing lights and a bustle of people in high visibility clothing. Paramedics promptly swooped on the three of them and they were bundled into the same ambulance for evaluation and treatment.

It turned out that they had all got off pretty lightly. Once Holda's cuts had been cleaned and taped up she was declared free to go. Father Jacobi needed a bandage for his head and was advised to rest for the remainder of the day. Rupert's arm was declared unbroken and put in a sling.

"Probably just a badly bruised collar bone," he grimaced ruefully when he was allowed to speak to the others. "The ambulance is going to drop me off at the doctor's surgery on its way back to base so I can get written off work. Anyone else need a lift to Büderich?"

Father Jacobi and Holda gladly took up the offer. They both accompanied Rupert to the doctor's surgery and waited while he was seen.

When he finally emerged he was looking relieved.

"It's definitely just a badly bruised rather than a broken collar bone," he reported. "It hurts like hell though. I wouldn't mind but I'm not allowed to drive for a few days." He stopped short and his face took on an expression of shock. "I wonder whether my car survived the tornado. I've left it back there, by the mill."

"My hotel's five minutes' walk from here. I'll drive you home, Father Jacobi," Holda suggested, "and then

Rupert and I can go and see about his car. I'd also like to know whether the manuscript survived the tornado, if it really was a twister."

"I was getting worried about the manuscript too," announced Father Jacobi. "I think I'll come with you back to Lank-Latum."

"But you're supposed to be resting, Father," protested Rupert, his voice reflecting annoyance rather than compassion.

"That's what paramedics always say to the elderly. I'll be fine. Come along children."

Half an hour later, Holda's Volkswagen inched into a parking space behind two fire-engines which were still at the scene of destruction. The whole of the top of the windmill appeared to have been torn off. The ground round about was strewn with masonry, smashed slates and the shattered remains of red-painted sails. A crowd of sightseers and photographers had gathered. At least one outside broadcast van was filming live footage in front of the fluttering police ribbon which served as a cordon. The cars next to Holda's all had heavily dented roofs and bonnets, and many had their front and rear windows smashed. When they found it, Rupert's vehicle was no exception.

"It's a complete write off," he groaned.

"This is why you have insurance," pointed out Holda. "Come on, let's put your recording gear into my car so we can drive it back to your place. Hello... where's Father Jacobi gone now? I thought he was right behind us."

They carried the assorted contents of Rupert's vehicle over to Holda's hatchback and then surveyed the scene.

"Look, there he is," called Rupert, pointing with his good hand to where the still dusty black figure of the priest was ducking under the police tape and walking briskly towards the entrance of the half wrecked mill.

"We'd better get after him," cried Holda urgently. "That book doesn't like him very much." At that moment, it didn't appear to be an odd statement to either of them.

They followed the priest's lead. As they ducked under the tape they heard a shout behind them, but they ran quickly towards the windmill door which was wide open. When they reached it they could already see Father Jacobi's figure standing amid the rubble, slightly to the left of centre in the circular function room. Jacobi turned and saw them. He took two steps towards them and instantly there was a deafening crash as the iron safe dropped the height of around four storeys onto the tiles below, landing exactly where the priest had been standing only a second earlier. Holda screamed and Rupert ran forward to grab the priest with his one good hand. Jacobi struggled and pulled himself away from Rupert's grasp. His face was white but determined, despite his narrow escape.

"Grab the book first!" he yelled.

The safe had partly cracked at the rear but was otherwise intact. Rupert turned the dial on the front, which was facing sideways, and the door swung free on one hinge. He reached in, caught up the book and passed it to Holda who had come up behind him. Together they fled the windmill where they were accosted by an officious policeman for breaching the safety tape. Rupert showed his city council credentials and lied that they had been ordered to retrieve an important item which was kept in the windmill, and which might otherwise be irretrievably damaged. The official was not mollified, but he let them go with just a blustery verbal warning.

Hastily, the three returned to Holda's car and with Father Jacobi in the front passenger seat, Rupert in the rear, and the book stowed in the hatchback, she pointed the vehicle in the direction of Büderich.

Chapter 7

It was Rupert who spoke first.

"Where exactly are we taking this accursed manuscript?"

"I thought we could put it in your office in the town hall again," began Holda, but then reconsidered. "But if you're off work for a week I won't be able to access it there. I'd rather not take it to the hotel. I don't like the idea of sleeping in the same room as the book."

Actually, I don't even want it in the same building as me, she thought to herself.

"Well, it's not coming home with me," asserted Rupert firmly. "I live in an apartment block with families. I'm not saying the manuscript caused that tornado just now but..." His voice tailed off. "I don't even like being in the same car with it," he admitted at last. "Do slow down, Holda," he added as an afterthought.

Holda obediently applied the brakes and slowed to a speed that would normally have shamed even a learner driver. A black Audi behind her honked impatiently until she let it overtake.

Father Jacobi had listened gravely to the conversation. "I'll be honest and say I don't like the whole thing either," he admitted. "Of course, it's probably all coincidence, that tornado and then the safe getting dislodged when it did. Still, we can't be too careful, given what we suspect we may be dealing with. It seems to me that the only viable place for the manuscript right now is my house. It's away from other buildings, so if anything happens it won't endanger other people. You can work in my study, Holda. I'll be around, so you won't be on your own with it. In the meantime, I can brush up on exorcism and purification rites and see if we can't contain any evil, if we cannot eliminate it completely. I can't allow this thing to be loose among my former parishioners. What do you say, Rupert? It's your call as the town archivist, as it's your archive's property."

"I don't like it at all," growled Rupert. "It seems to me that the manuscript has its strongest vendetta against you personally, Papa. Maybe because you are a priest."

"Do you have a better idea?"

"I don't. I just wish there was somewhere different we could take it."

They drove on in silence until they reached Father Jacobi's little house by the Rhine. Now that it was daylight, Holda could see that it was an attractive, old, two storey house with a steep sloping roof, half-timbered with an old red brick infill, and with a flourishing vegetable and herb garden to the side. Giant savoy cabbages and rows of onions filled the beds, and runner bean plants, gleaming with scarlet flowers, snaked up bamboo wigwams next to the house. Rosemary, sage, thyme, borage, chives, mint, parsley and a range of other herbs which Holda could not recognise spilled out over the sides of giant stone planters around the house itself. Further back were some old sheds and a disused barn.

"It's very fertile soil round here, as we're next to the flood plain," explained Jacobi, following Holda's gaze. "I grow as much of my own food as I can. In point of fact, I made a big pot of thick vegetable soup yesterday. Come on in and have some. We missed lunch!"

In a short time the three of them were seated at Father Jacobi's kitchen table savouring steaming bowls of the priest's fragrant herbal broth. Alongside it he served thick chunks of dark home-baked bread, spread generously with fresh garlicky butter. The manuscript lay on a desk in the next room, thankfully out of their line of sight. Holda ate eagerly and as her hunger subsided she also felt the stinging of her various injuries begin to lessen.

"Remind me again, Holda," asked Father Jacobi once he was half way down his bowl of soup, "what research you need the actual presence of the manuscript for?"

Holda decided to confess.

"I need to make a transcript and translation of it," she explained. "I actually took photographs of all the writing on the first day, so I can do that without the presence of the book itself." She hesitated, remembering the vellum pages at the back of the book. "But there are some blank pages behind the diary part which…" Again she stopped. She was going to sound unhinged. "Where I imagined I saw something written," she whispered. "When I looked again there was nothing there but Azriel told me to keep a special watch on those leaves. He knows more than he's letting on, I'm sure of it."

"Well, if you have photographs of the pages, we can split the work between us," suggested Jacobi brightly. "My Latin is as good as anyone's. Back in the day I used to teach it at the Jesuit seminary, so I can transcribe the botanical and astronomical sections. You're the only one who can read Middle High German, so you can do the diary and, if you don't mind working from the original, you can keep an eye on those blank pages while you're at it. If we start now we'll be through by not long after midnight. Rupert can go home and rest his shoulder."

"I'm not going anywhere," protested Rupert. "I'll stay here and make sure you're both safe. At minimum I can keep a kettle boiling and a weather eye out for any demons you accidentally raise."

Nobody laughed at his joke.

Ten minutes later, Father Jacobi was seated at the kitchen table with Holda's laptop in front of him, sporting a pair of wire-framed reading glasses and scribbling Latin sentences onto a thick pad of paper. The bandage round his head gave him the odd air of an ancient sage. Holda was seated at the desk by the living room window, transcribing the diary into her notebook, her pen alternating between hovering motionless over the page and then scribbling in a frenzy once a sentence had been deciphered. Rupert, meanwhile, was scouring Father Jacobi's bookshelves for something to pass the time. He selected the first non-ecclesiastical tome he could find - a volume of Heroes and Legends of the Rhine - and then settled down on the sofa to read. It promised to be a long, weary evening. They had agreed to reconvene every two hours to update each other on their progress and to take a short break over a glass of Father Jacobi's home-made rhubarb and ginger wine.

After a few minutes, Rupert moved to the kitchen and sat reading at the far side of the kitchen table. He seemed to want to put distance between himself and the book. Every so often he glanced over towards the living room with an almost angry look on his face. Ten minutes later he returned to the living room again.

He was visibly agitated and seemed unable to settle or concentrate on anything.

By the time the first break came around, Holda already had twinges of cramp in the fingers of her right hand. They convened around the wood burner in the living room. The priest poured out three small glasses of a pinkish golden liquid. It tasted sweet but at the same time tart and fiery. It restored their mood from the first sip onwards. Even Rupert seemed slightly happier.

"This tastes good," he admitted grudgingly. "I'd be amazed if old von Deibel has any recipe to match this," he added. "Alright Father, you start with your update."

"I'm still on the first section," announced Jacobi, suddenly serious. "It starts off with specific recipes for a whole set of potions, which I've noted down here. There are cures for boils, herpes, gout, tumours and melancholia among other ailments. All the remedies sound nasty and are certainly ineffectual. There are also sleeping draughts, love potions and poisons. Some of them come with incantations, but most seem to work without them. Then there's a section on specific ingredients. This is where it gets particularly grisly. There are around two dozen recipes for different magic philtres which use the blood, brains and so on of dead infants. For instance, if someone eats a pie made from the tongues of babies who had not yet learned to talk, it says they can never be made to confess to any sorcery even if tortured, which must have been relevant at the time of the witch trials. After eating these speechless tongues, no witch in the coven would be able to articulate the names of the other members and so betray them. Apart from that, there are specific instructions on the method of draining blood from a murdered child's corpse. This fresh child-blood by the way, is claimed to be a powerful truth serum when drained into a chalice and allowed to fall onto the naked flesh of a person lying on the demonic altar."

He paused, his forehead beaded with perspiration, then took a sip of wine, which appeared to restore him. Holda and Rupert pecked at theirs too.

"Other ingredients discussed include toads, rats and crows. There's also a half page on baby fat, which seems to be considered a supreme ingredient in all kinds of elixirs. Adult corpses are used to heal skin eruptions, tumours, birthmarks and gout, which can all be stroked away using a dead hand. For toothache the finger of a dead child is said to be more effective. Some recipes are intended for use at the celebration of the black Mass. For instance, it says the arm of a baby which has not yet been baptised may be used as a candle. It says here that the ends of the fingers can be lit and will burn with five clear flames. It's known as the Hand of Glory."

He paused and peered at them over his spectacles.

"That's as far as I have got," he announced. "So far it's a sort of foul witch's cookbook. That bit about the gruesome candle is interesting though. The same thing is described in the Grimoire of Pope Honorius, which was widely thought to be a sixteenth century fake. This document is decidedly older, so probably that superstition does indeed date from the medieval period."

Henrietta's missing hand, thought Holda to herself. I wonder whether that was taken to cure somebody's acne or gout.

She pointed at the bound volume which lay open, two feet away from her on the table.

"My section's no better," she sighed. "Johannes von Deibel was dead serious about wanting to raise the devil and beget the Anti-Christ."

She read aloud first the section she had already transcribed which outlined his origins, education and intent to capture young Marieken of Pesch for the hideous ceremony twelve days hence. Then came the new section:

Only twelve days remain to me before my Lord and Master returns to this place. Twelve days which will decide my fate. Either I fail in my sworn purpose and my soul will be forfeit to Lord Satan for exquisite excrucia-tion lasting all eternity, or I will succeed in my design. Then our child will rise on Earth as the Anti-Christ to destroy mankind and lay waste to the foul angelic legions of Saint Michael, and banish God and his weakling son forever to their crumbling rotten paradise. For this is the bargain I made with my Lord Satan when he released me from the torture of the accursed monks of Kaiserswerth, and this contract I myself signed using a raven's quill dipped in a vial of my own blood.

Lord Satan gave me the means to travel. He also bestowed riches and fine clothes on me, and guided me to the greatest teachers of his arts. From them and from their books and scrolls have I learned the arts of the Sabbat, the skills of the Haruspex, the visions of the astronomer and the necromancer. I can boil up the stews and pastes which can kill or cure. I know the magical properties of all body parts of the newly stran-gled unbaptized babe. I know the power of the unsus-pecting virgin to lure demons and yes, even Lucifer himself who lusts more than any after such sweet dainties, always longing to impregnate them through his hairy loins.

The sweet Marieken of Haus Pesch is the choicest morsel of all. Her beauty is beyond compare in all Germany. She is devout, chaste, innocent of all sin. Her name means little Maria in our local parlance; the very same name as the mother of that invertebrate who let himself be nailed to a cross instead of smiting down his enemies. I shall enable Lucifer to plunder Marieken's maidenhood and force her to bear the very whelp which will end mankind's reign on this Earth. That will be the price of my eternal power and glory as Satan's right hand servant, nay I dare even say, his equal.

Holda looked up from her writing. Jacobi swiftly crossed himself, while looking sidelong at Rupert and then back at her.

"Forgive me, Father," she blurted. "I'm only repeating what is written in the manuscript."

"I know, child, I know. We do need to understand as much about it as we can in order to counter its evil. I know these are not your words, but those of the vilest monster that ever lived. Don't forget that when your voice repeats his filth and blasphemy and your pen etches his words onto the paper, his corruption is lessened by the purity of your soul. You are weakening the evil as you read. Please do go on."

I don't believe that for one moment, thought Holda. By speaking these words aloud I'm just inducting two more people into their wicked secrets. But she read on anyway:

In twelve days the planets will be aligned in such a way as we have not seen for more than two hundred years.

The red planet Mars will be close to the Earth in the aura of a giant moon. A lunar eclipse will take place at exactly the hour of midnight from Thursday to Friday, the day of the witches' Sabbat. In that moment, as the sky goes dark, shall Satan appear and violate the sweet Marieken until her screams cause the sheeted dead to gibber in their very graves.

"Hello!" exclaimed Rupert suddenly. "I read about something like that. There will be a super moon constellation and lunar eclipse just like that sometime this year. It was in the paper last week. It's probably not as rare as he claims."

Holda acknowledged his words with a glance and then continued:

Everything is prepared. Marieken will be kept hidden in my tower until the night of the eclipse. She will not be harmed in this time, but she must be kept silent and restrained. I will feed and water her well in this time for she will need her strength. Then, on the afternoon before the chosen night, I will drug her with the sleeping draught whose recipe is written in my notes and carry her to the sacred place. I will strip her naked and place her, bound in straps made of hanged men's skin, across the altar where burn the Hand of Glory candles. Her legs will be splayed and her luscious cunny opened and ready to receive my master. Waving a phial of toad's breath near her face will bring her back to her wits, though it must only be a slight whiff as everything from a toad is venomous. As she regains consciousness, I shall utter the ancient cabbalistic incantation of the false popes and my Lord Satan himself will seize possession of my body and use my very own loins to ravish the wench.

Holda looked up again and saw that Rupert and the priest were both hanging on her every word agog. As soon as they caught her eye, both looked down swiftly at the carpet in embarrassed confusion.

"Well, I think another half glass of rhubarb and ginger after that," broke in Jacobi at last. "It really is a dreadful old book isn't it?"

They were both thoroughly enjoying the story, thought Holda. Relishing it even. They're behaving like I've caught them listening to violent pornography. I saw the lascivious expression on their faces. While I was reading they were playing the scene like a film in their minds. This book is the most blasphemous and vile thing ever written. It brings out the worst in everyone who goes near it. I will email back to Azriel and tell him I'm not doing it any more.

She took a gulp of wine and then realised: but Azriel has the power to kick me off my doctorate course. Do I even have the option of stopping with this task, if I ever want to complete my thesis? She gave a deep sigh. Perhaps it's just me overthinking everything as usual. Or maybe the manuscript's influence is making me suspect the worst of Rupert and Father Jacobi. All these events took place over six hundred years ago. Whether I transcribe the text or not can make no difference to anything now. She drained her glass and turned reluctantly back to the manuscript while Rupert and the priest retreated to the kitchen.

They had scarcely resumed their seats when a sudden scream from Holda brought them running back to the living room.

"What's wrong? What happened?" demanded Rupert, snaking an arm around her shoulders.

Holda was staring at the manuscript, her face drained of blood, her mouth hanging open, daring neither to move nor breathe. The pages were flipped over to where the blank section started. There on the page, the Middle High German words: 'Kom mich ze helf' were now plainly visible in black on the tan coloured vellum.

Chapter 8

It was a long time before anyone spoke. Then it was Father Jacobi who pronounced, "This book is truly dangerous. I would never have believed it. But if the church believes in holy miracles then surely the reverse, the very blackest of magic phenomena, is also within the realms of the possible."

"But who is it, speaking to us?" hissed Holda. "How do the letters appear? It can't really be magic, can it? It must be a trick. Perhaps it's invisible ink. Maybe the words appeared with the warmth of the fire. But what does it mean? Who needed help and why?" She shuddered, thinking of the scenario conjured up by Johannes von Deibel's diary. It wasn't hard to imagine someone pleading for help if he were involved.

"Hold the book near the stove and see if any more words appear," suggested Rupert. Holda did as he proposed, but none of the vellum pages revealed any writing other than those four ominous words at the top of the first leaf.

"It has been sent to try to distract us from our purpose," announced Father Jacobi firmly. "We will ignore it and complete our transcription."

I don't think that's it at all, thought Holda to herself. It was trying to say the same thing to me at the windmill. But maybe the priest is right about carrying on. Maybe the answer to the riddle really is in the manuscript somewhere.

They returned to their respective tasks but this time Rupert chose to remain in the same room as Holda, perched with his book on the sofa. She could hear him fidgeting as he flipped the pages. She found it difficult to concentrate now on the faded sepia script. Even though her back was turned towards him, Holda felt that Rupert was only pretending to read. She could feel him watching her with those uncannily blue eyes of his.

I wonder what he's thinking about, she thought. Is he visualising Marieken spread-eagled on the satanic altar? Am I imagining it or is he really staring at me? What expression would I see on his face if I turned around? Why am I afraid to look?

She forced herself to focus on the pages in front of her and she was soon fiercely scratching out words in her jotter again.

When they next reconvened it was already nearly ten. Father Jacobi insisted on rinsing their wine glasses in the kitchen. While he did so, Holda sat awkwardly avoiding eye contact with Rupert, while at the same time trying not to appear rude.

As a diversion she spoke. "How's the book of Rhine legends?"

"Interesting. I've been learning about Cologne cathedral and how the architect made a pact with the devil in order to get such a wonderful design for it."

"Not Satan again," sighed Holda, irked. "That brute seems to be popping up everywhere."

"In the Cologne case, the architect manages to outwit the fiend and his soul is saved." Rupert sounded hurt at Holda's tone. "In fact, Rhineland folk seem to have specialised in bamboozling the devil. The swordsmith of Solingen cheated Lucifer too and even managed to steal the secret of making Damascus blades from him."

"If only Johannes von Deibel had been more like that. He just seems like a great sadistic pervert, hell-bent on abducting and raping poor little Marieken," commented Holda pointedly.

Before Rupert could respond, Father Jacobi bustled in with the glasses and poured them each a portion of wine.

"I'm pretty much finished with the first two sections," he announced. "I'm fortunate as the Latin handwriting's much easier than that in Holda's diary part. I haven't transcribed everything, but I have skimmed it through and understood everything. Basically the first text continues in the same vein as we saw before, but focused on curses and poisons, especially using parts of the viper. There's a longish section on the use of symbols and invocations in the black Mass to summon the fiend. The second piece is largely copied from the texts of ancient astrologers and talks about the properties and auspices of the planets, as well as their movements. There's an interesting part where he calculates future movements and alignments of the planets and constellations. By that I mean future from the date of his writing. I have no way of checking the accuracy of his calculations, but it ties in with the description you translated for us two hours ago. The date when he aimed to raise the devil was the night of April 30th to May 1st 1361.

"That's Walpurgis night!" exclaimed Rupert. "The night when witches celebrated orgiastic rites on the Brocken, the tallest peak in the Harz mountains. It's the old German version of Halloween."

"Not just on the Brocken," replied the priest. "Every region had a mountain or forest where the covens would celebrate Walpurgis night. Around here it would have been done in the forest, as we're in the flatlands. The main thing was always to hold these blasphemous ceremonies far away from the prying eyes of any fellow citizens. In those days it was downright dangerous to be seen to worship Satan. Even a baseless accusation of it could get you hanged or burnt at the stake."

"The diary also carries on in the same dreadful vein as the earlier stuff," reported Holda. "I'm not sure I'll get through it all tonight, but here's the next part anyway. This entry was obviously written a few days after the previous one."

It is done. I have the maiden in my possession.

That village simpleton Wil Biskup thwarted my plan for three days by following Marieken like a hound as she went down to the smithy, to the beekeeper's sheds and to the chapel. Today I made sure to greet the idiot boy as he hung about the gates of Haus Pesch. I offered him a sweet cake into which I had baked a powerful sleeping potion. The halfwit followed his Marieken into the forest when she went to gather wild bears' garlic and there he shared the cake with her. The two of them lay down under a tree and fell asleep like children. It was the simplest matter after that for me to lift up the tasty sleeping wench and carry her here to my tower. I have gagged her and tied her hand and foot to the bedpost in my garret. But now I must leave off writing and make haste to the village in the guise of a traveller. I wish to observe the stout villagers whipping Wil Biskup in the stocks this afternoon. The good burghers

disbelieve his account of the wench's disappearance,
and think that by flaying his hide he will tell them where
Marieken or her corpse may be found. I will watch from
in the crowd behind him so that he does not see me and
denounce me as the one who gave him the cake. That
will also afford me the best view of his flinching flesh.

Holda looked up from her notebook.

"Johannes von Deibel, the gift that keeps on giving,"
she spat out savagely. "Just when you thought he
couldn't get any worse. Listen to the next entry, which
must have been from the following day."

Every moment spent in Marieken's company is pure
delight to me. Yesterday evening I went to the chamber
where she is confined naked and brought her a piece of
black bread and a pitcher of water. I removed the gag
from her face and straightway she began to screech like
a bahkauv. At this I slapped her and bade her be silent
lest I give her proper cause to squeal."

"Sorry, I have no idea what a bahkauv is," Holda interrupted her narrative.

"It features in the book I'm reading. It's a sort of
legendary Rhineland monster shaped like a calf, but
with fangs," explained Rupert, his face agog. "Go on,
Holda..."

I held the pitcher to her lips and let her moisten them.
Then I lifted my tunic and showed her the long pikestaff
between my loins and asked her how she might best like
it. She squealed again like a pig at slaughter, so I fetched
up a bundle of birch twigs and warmed her loins with

them for a goodly time until they glowed like coals, though I was careful not to break the skin. I told her then about how the villagers had flogged the simpleton Wil Biskup until he fell in a swoon. She wept and snivelled so deliciously that my fleshy ladyware rose up hard. I was sore tempted to relieve her of her maidenhead, but to do so would bring such vengeance of my Lord Satan upon me that I dared not touch her cunny. Instead I made her kiss my rod and take it between her lips and quench her thirst on my hot fluid, and all the while I told her that she would be spared a ravishing if only she sucked me well. I have returned twice since to her chamber and each time she has served the wants of my loins most diligently in return for a little water and bread. Her maidenhood remains intact.

But I may not dally longer with the sweet wench. I must continue my preparations for my master's coming. The place is to be deep in the forest half a league from the settlement at Ossum. There stands a great flat rock which serves as our altar. The covens of Budderich, Strimpf and Bischke are to be present. I must prepare the materials, candles and potions secretly and transport them there, so that as night falls we may quickly dedicate the altar with incantations and symbols for this momentous act of conception. Once night has come and the company is gathered I shall fetch the sleeping maid and place her face downward across the slab. Her wrists will be bound. Her legs will be spread apart and tied with skin-thongs to two stakes driven into the ground. Then I will awaken the wench and summon our Dark Lord who will rise from the pit and drive the very soul from my carcass. Taking possession of my body, he will commit the act of impregnation. Then he *will gouge out the tongue of the maiden, that she may never reveal the lineage of the whelp conceived on that night. When my Lord returns me to my own anatomy he will give the dumb maid into my charge again and I shall nurture her tenderly until the cub is born, and for one year after that until it is weaned. I must take great care that nought befalls the child. The mother though shall be my plaything. When the child is a year old, I shall take the babe away and leave Marieken in the tower to starve.*

"That's as far as I got," finished Holda, shuddering involuntarily. "That horrible part about the gouged tongue is spooky though. It sounds exactly like what happened with Henrietta von Hüls. Except something must have gone wrong in Henrietta's case, because she didn't survive the experience. And her head and right hand were cut off too."

"Given the predilection for using human body parts in their concoctions, it's not hard to see why a hand might be carried off in the Middle Ages," mused Jacobi gravely. "But in Henrietta's case it would mean these diabolical medieval customs were still being practiced up to the early nineteenth century. I find that hard to believe."

"Father," pleaded Holda weakly, "I need to go outside for some fresh air. I have to get away from the book for a while. I'll walk up to the bench and look at the Rhine in the moonlight."

"I'll come with you," offered Rupert.

He spoke too eagerly, thought Holda. His blue eyes remained on her face for longer than felt comfortable. As she returned his gaze, his tongue flicked out and moistened his lips.

"I think Father Jacobi should come too," she entreated. "I don't like the idea of the book getting access to him all on his own. It might burn his house down or something while we're gone, with him inside it. The manuscript is safe enough here on its own. And if it isn't...at least we'll all be out of the house if any lightning bolt strikes."

The priest won't realise it but he's my chaperone tonight, thought Holda. There's been something creepy about Rupert ever since I read out those evil thoughts of Johannes von Deibel. I wonder if he gets turned on by that sort of thing. How did I ever find those eyes attractive? When they look at me now I see only anger and lust. I need to know exactly what he's thinking before I drive him home tonight. I don't want to be alone with him in the car, but I don't suppose I can refuse to take him with his arm in a sling. Perhaps if I drink more of the wine I can say I can't drive and we can take a taxi. I don't want to stay in this house any longer though. I can't face that book any more tonight.

They put on their coats and walked out onto the dyke path. A half-moon was intermittently visible between eerie strands of cloud which cold, hard gusts of wind were chasing over the black sky. Whenever the half-orb appeared, the Rhine glittered back a diagonal reflection like a shining path, as though inviting them to plunge into its icy waters.

Holda shivered and walked on faster. The other two quickened their pace to keep up with her. When they reached the bench the reflection of the moon stretched away from directly in front of them.

"There's only one bench on the whole path," observed Holda. "I wonder why they put it here, not at the bend in the river where you can see in both directions."

She sat down on the bench and her two companions seated themselves on either side of her.

"The story of the bench is a tragic one," explained Father Jacobi slowly. "The original bench was placed here in 1959 by the father of a young woman who had drowned herself in the Rhine at this point. He used to come here to sit and remember her. In 1960, exactly a year after her suicide, he also took his own life at this spot."

"What an awful, sad tale," sighed Holda. "I wonder what can have driven her to it."

"I've heard versions of this story from several people I've interviewed for the archives," chimed in Rupert. "The girl's name was Gisela Hahn. She was sixteen when she died and she had been really popular in the village; a lively character, very pretty, but with a reputation for being rather flirty. She was extremely popular with the local boys as you can imagine. She was an only child whose mother was dead, and her father was said by some to be very strict and by others to be over-protective. He was a proper stalwart of the community, a churchgoer, a member of the town council and a committee member of several local clubs."

How similar Rupert's job is to that of a priest, thought Holda to herself. He too teases out the stories from the locals. He listens to their accounts and tries to make sense of them. He collects and hoards and catalogues snippets of other people's lives. But he doesn't tease out the deeper secrets. He doesn't ask what they really did or thought. He lets them sanitize their accounts. If he does stumble across inconvenient details, like the Nazi mural, he hides them. He can't judge people properly because he never hears the real truth about them. If he did know, I wonder what he would do with the information.

"So why did Gisela drown herself?" asked Holda.

"She was pregnant. Nobody really knows the details. Presumably she either had a lover, or else she flirted with someone and things got out of hand and she was raped. Most likely she didn't want to tell her father, or else she did tell him and he took it badly. He blamed himself for her death, that's for sure. He came up here on the anniversary of her death, on the second of May 1960, and shot himself."

"What here? On this very bench?" Holda jumped up in alarm.

"The original bench fell into disrepair and the church authorities have replaced it twice since," explained Father Jacobi dryly. "I organised that myself. It was…the right thing to do under the circumstances," he added.

"And ever since, you've kept a suicide watch on people sitting out here?" observed Holda with admiration in her voice.

"I can see the bench from the window in my loft. I often sit up there at dusk and keep a watch through my field glasses. If I see someone who looks like they might be suicidal I come up here and talk to them. Mostly though, it's just young couples in love who walk out here and use the bench. It's always deserted here after dusk. I'm certain over the years that I've seen the conception of at least seven children of the parish taking place on this seat." He chuckled to himself. Holda looked down at him sharply. She suddenly felt an unexpected surge of anger coursing through her veins.

You filthy old bastard, she thought. The suicide watch story is all a ruse. You're just a dirty peeping Tom. You even had the bench replaced so your evening live show wouldn't be interrupted. I wonder why you really came out to befriend me and invite me straight back to your place. Was that pastoral care or was it an attempt at grooming me? And of course I trusted you because you were dressed in a priest's dog-collar. How could I be so naïve? As though the papers haven't been full for years of stories of priests who turn out to be sex abusers. Look at the expression on his face when he looks at me. Does he know what I'm thinking? Say something Holda, say something to distract his attention.

"Did you know Gisela Hahn, Father?" she asked. "Did you hear her confession?"

"I knew her, of course," replied Jacobi slowly. "But no priest ever reveals the secrets of the confessional. It is our job to keep everyone's secrets. As it happens, Gisela was in the same school class as me. I was only sixteen when she died, and of course I wasn't a priest then. Far from it," he added almost to himself as an afterthought.

"It's getting cold," butted in Rupert. "We should be getting back. Would you give me a lift back to my flat, Holda?"

"Do you have a spare bed at your flat?" asked Holda, catching his sidelong look as the moon emerged from behind a cloud.

The tongue moistened the lips again.

"Of course," Rupert's lips spoke with a slightly lop-sided smile, "I have a lovely, quiet guest room and I always keep it made up, just in case."

"Great. You can put Father Jacobi up in there then. It's not safe to leave him alone in the house with that book. Also, someone should keep an eye on that head injury of his."

"Of course I'll be fine in my own house!" protested Father Jacobi.

"But what if you're not?" retorted Holda. "That book already tried to kill you twice this afternoon, first with the tornado and then when it fell down in the safe from the top of the windmill. We'll finish transcribing and translating the text tomorrow and I can send it all to Azriel. Then we'll find somewhere to lock the thing away. A bank vault maybe. I'll call round for you both at ten tomorrow morning." She turned her most winning smile on Rupert. "You'll put Father Jacobi up in your spare room, won't you Rupert? Please say you will."

Rupert looked highly put-out by Holda's words, but there was no reasonable objection to be mustered.

The three strolled back to the priest's house where Jacobi quickly tossed together an overnight bag. Then they all climbed into Holda's car and set off. She dropped the two off in front of Rupert's apartment block on the south side of Büderich, then took herself to her hotel. As she parked, she noticed something lying on the back seat. She looked round and saw that it was a dark coloured book. Holda let out a terrified scream. Then she began to laugh hysterically.

It's only Rupert's copy of the Rhine Legends, she thought to herself, almost crying with relief. I'll borrow it tonight. It might help me settle down to sleep, after all that's happened today. In the end it might not be a bad idea to learn more about people outwitting Satan.

I think I might even have cheated a couple of randy devils myself this evening.

As she lay in bed with the reading lamp on, she opened the first page of Rupert's book. The first story was about Saint Wilgefortis, whose name, she learned, derives from the Latin *virgo fortis*, meaning strong virgin. As a young girl, Wilgefortis was chased through a forest by a group of men intent on deflowering her. In her terror she prayed to the virgin Mary for help. Her prayer was answered. At that moment she came to a huge wayside cross, such as you see all over Europe. Wilgefortis placed herself in front of the cross with her arms stretched out. As her pursuers ran up, a beard suddenly grew on her face and the wicked gang ran on past, mistaking her for an effigy of Christ crucified. Since then, from the Rhineland to Austria, you can find images which appear to show a bearded but distinctly female Jesus nailed to the cross.

She shut the book with a snap and clicked off the light. If sending miraculous facial hair is the virgin Mary's best response, I'm going to have to answer my own prayers, she thought.

Chapter 9

Holda was running through a dark forest with a pack of wolves behind her, drawing ever closer, always gaining on her. Then she realised with a shock that these wolves were sprinting upright on powerful hairy thighs, running like satyrs with wolves' heads. As one drew alongside her, its jaws were slavering and its fetid breath was hot and stifling. She saw with a shock that its eyes were a bright, clear, blue colour. At the same time her face was prickling with a sudden and alarming growth of whiskers. She awoke to the sound of her own voice shrieking out for help in Middle High German.

Footsteps sounded outside her door and a voice in German called out, asking whether she was alright.

"Yes, sorry. I just had a bad dream," she answered back. "I'm fine."

The footsteps disappeared off down the corridor.

Holda got up and went to the bathroom. Then she came back and fired up her laptop. There were five messages from Azriel. She opened the first one:

Transcribe the details of the planetary alignment von Deibel used. Send this to me at once. Azriel.

The second email had arrived around an hour later:

Leave the potions section for now. After the astronomical part, focus on the diary. Send sections as you go along. Keep your eye on the blank pages and report at once if you see anything. You will know. Azriel.

The third email from two hours later sounded annoyed:

Remember to check your mailbox frequently and acknowledge my messages. I need you to respond to my emails dammit. A.

Then a fourth email from the evening:

There was a report on the news about a tornado in Meerbusch. Please confirm that the manuscript is safe and undamaged. Azriel.

He doesn't ask whether I am safe and undamaged, noted Holda.

The fifth email from near midnight caused her to gasp in panic:

Flying into Düsseldorf at midday tomorrow. Clearly going there in person is the only way to get any answers to my questions. Be at the hotel with the manuscript at one. If that idiot Keller won't give you the book, leave an address at reception where I can find you and it. Or deign to answer my email with the details. Send whatever transcriptions you have already done, so I can read them on the plane. Fucking do this now. Azriel.

Holda got dressed quickly, sat down again at her laptop and typed up her transcriptions from the previous day. She also wrote a quick summary of what she could remember of Father Jacobi's words. Then she searched through her photographs of the Latin section and found the pages dealing with the planetary alignment. She added them as an attachment to her email and pressed send.

Let him translate the old devil's planetary calculations for himself, she thought viciously. I can understand the Latin, but I don't know anything about astronomy or the names of constellations. Father Jacobi seemed far more clued up about all that. He and Azriel can figure it out together. Then, as an afterthought, Holda sent another email which read:

I was working on the manuscript at the Teloy windmill when the tornado struck. The mill's roof and sails were destroyed and Rupert Keller and I were both injured, along with a local retired priest, Father Jacobi. The book is safe. For now it is at Father Jacobi's house by the Rhine. The address is Am Rheinpfad 6. Some writing appeared on the first of the blank pages but it makes no sense. It's just four words asking for help.

Holda looked at the clock in the corner of her screen. Seven thirty. If she was quick she might finish the transcript before it was time to pick up Rupert and Father Jacobi. She scrolled through the photos until she came to the point her previous translation had reached.

Everything is ready for tomorrow night.
I am in such a turmoil I can scarcely contain my passion. I have visited Marieken five times today, that she might quell my lust with her dainty lips. She suspects nothing about what awaits her. She has become obedient to my commands. I have not had cause to

birch her again, though I shall do so for my own enjoy-
ment once she has born my master's babe. Until then
I must treat her gently enough that she may not
miscarry and bring Satan's wrath down on us.

That imbecile Wil Biskup has been released and is
roaming the woods in search of Marieken. He moves
about stiffly and painfully. It is but seven days since he
was whipped and his hide is not yet healed. I must
be wary of him. If he sees me he will recognize me as the
one who gave him the drugged cake. He shouts her
name aloud. If he comes close by here she may try to
answer him. I must be vigilant and ensure Marieken is
at all times gagged, either with a cloth or with my own
flesh sword stuffed in her mouth. The gouging of the
wench's tongue cannot come too soon.

Holda stood up and began to pace around the room.

I can hardly believe such a monster existed, she
thought. But then again, he's probably only as bad as
Jack the Ripper or a dozen other modern serial rapists
and killers. I remember the way he was scapegoated by
the monks when he was a child, and how they murdered
his poor hermaphrodite parent. That's why he wants to
starve Marieken to death. If they'd had psychiatrists
back then they'd have had a field day with this case.
Is nature or nurture more at fault here?

She resumed her seat. The next entry was written in a
different shade of brown ink and the writing was even
shakier than before.

All is lost! I am undone! The wench is dead.

My preparations were competed to perfection. All
members of the covens were arrived. The altar was

furnished, the Hands of Glory lit, inverted pentacles and magic circles traced out on the ground in white stones, and the symbol of chaos daubed on the forehead of everyone present.

My sleeping draught worked its purpose and I bore the sleeping maiden to the gathering and placed her on the rock. I bound her hands together with leather straps made from the skin of hanged men. More of these thongs I used to position her legs spread wide apart, tied to two thick poles hammered deep into the ground for this purpose. The members of the covens were drunk and leery on juniper wine and some of the men pleasured themselves openly at the sight of the maiden's cunny-hole, but none dared to take her. That privilege would be saved for our dark lord.

I began the black chant to invoke our master and at the same time, approaching the altar, uncorked a small bottle in which I had earlier suffocated a living toad. The vial was filled with the exhaled breath of the reptile. As I passed it near Marieken's face, the stench of toad's breath revived her and she began to scream. This made the assembly jeer and laugh and I had to bid them be silent so I could finish my incantation. As I finished, the maid's screams had faded to floods of weeping. At that moment, in a cloud of stinking vapour, my Lord arose shaped like a giant satyr with a goat's legs and horns, a man's torso, and a face so terrible as to make all present avert their gaze. Between his thighs rose aloft a pudding-prick as long as a sword and as thick as a grown man's arm.

"Possess me Master," I beseeched him. "Use my body and let me plant your seed into the wench."

But my master laughed at me with such a roar that the trees all around us shook and some lost their leaves.

"*Should I use your puny body when I have my own?*" *he bellowed back at me.* "*Fool that you are. I have no need of a knave for this. I sow my seed from my own mighty prick alone.*"

So saying, he fell upon the wench and rammed his meaty stave so hard into her that I feared she might be split in two. The coven members likewise jumped upon each other and the whole forest rocked with the sound of lusty fornication. Marieken shrieked so loud, impaled there on the devil's own prick, that her cries must have been heard across the river in Kaiserswerth. I myself ploughed the furrow of a hideous old woman from Bischke whose naked breasts sagged down almost to her cunny, but I was sore aggrieved to have missed deflowering the sweet Marieken. After he had finished with her, the dark prince strode around the altar and, laughing in a voice like thunder, reached out two of his clawed fingers and ripped the tongue from her very mouth.

He placed the organ into his own jaws and chewed it, letting the blood drip from the corners of his chops. As he swallowed it, a foul stinking cloud of vapour enveloped him and when it had cleared he was gone, leaving the wench howling on the altar, with blood pouring from her lips and her defiled cunny.

I went forward now, for some of the men were close approaching and they would all have impaled the wounded damsel in turn if I had not hindered them. If I could not be the first, I resolved I should at least be second to mount the mare.

I untied her and carried her from that place in the direction of my tower. When I was far from the site of the ceremony and on a dark path through the forest, something hard struck me from behind on the head. I staggered and let the maid fall. I was struck again from behind. I span round and saw the simpleton, Wil Biskup, holding a rock which he smashed into my face, breaking my nose and filling my eyes with blood. Blinded, I tried to hit him with my hand but my fist struck only empty air. By the time I had wiped the blood from my eyes and could part way see again, he was disappearing through the trees with the shrieking wench thrown over his shoulder like a sack of meal.

I gave chase, wounded as I was. He would have been quicker but he was weighed down by his howling burden. Nonetheless, it was all I could do not to lose sight of them. His burden was getting heavier though and by the time they reached the shore of the Rhine I was very close behind. At that part of the riverbank there was a fisherman's rowing boat on the stony shore. Wil Biskup threw the naked wench down into the vessel and began to tug it to the water with all his might. As he got it afloat I arrived, waded into the stream and caught hold of the stern. He hit me with an oar and I lost my balance. That gave him time to skull the coracle out into the faster flowing part of the river. I swam after and caught the boat again. This time I was quick. I managed to pull myself over the edge of the boat. The girl was screeching from the bloody hole in her face. I made a grab at her but Biskup pulled her back by the arm. The boat rocked violently and the pair of them went overboard into the river.

Biskup made it back to shore alive. Using the boat I searched for Marieken but she was vanished. Her drowned corpse was found next day washed up on the shore near the village of Ordingen.

All is lost. My master will track me down and I shall be held to account for the catastrophic loss of the maid and his newly conceived offspring. But I will outfox him yet. The first thing that must be done is for me to plan my revenge on those idiots. Wil Biskup has been captured and hauled before the magistrates. His story is not believed and he is to be hanged tomorrow on the heath by Crefeld for abducting, deflowering and torturing the maid. The drowned wench was buried yesterday morning in the churchyard at Strimpf with all due ceremony, and at midnight I went to her grave with my spade, exhumed her corpse and fetched it here to my tower. She is lying here next to me as I write. The only sport left to me when I finish my notes will be to defile her cold, dead corpse. I am inscribing this last entry using an ink mixed with my own blood. Tonight I shall strip off the fair, soft skin from her thighs, buttocks, stomach and back to make pages of vellum. When I cut down the hanged corpse of Wil Biskup from the gallows on the heath, I shall take his skin too and bind into a single book all the vellum pages, my magic recipes and other notes, along with this journal. I have knowledge of an incantation which traps the souls of those whose skin or blood are used in making a book. Any who use their blood hereafter to write on these pages may similarly be denied access to Heaven and spared the inferno. We three will haunt this volume for all eternity, and no power known to man nor even to the beast himself can release us. So long as this tome exists I shall escape an eternity in the hottest pits of Hell, and those fools Marieken von Pesch and Wil Biskup cannot be admitted into Paradise. May our suspended souls haunt anyone who reads these words.

Holda sat back, exhaled deeply and stared at her note-book. Her stomach was churning and her mind racing.

The book is actually bound in Wil Biskup's skin, she thought. Those blank pages at the back are the six hundred year old epidermis of a murdered girl. That in itself makes the thing horrific, let alone the vile diary and diabolical spells. What on earth does Azriel want with this ghastly thing?

Holda shuddered suddenly at the shocking revelation that entered her brain.

"He wants to know the right planetary alignment," she gasped out loud. "That means he wants to calculate which is the right day to summon the devil."

Her eye caught the clock in the corner of her laptop screen. Half past nine. It was time to pick up Rupert and Father Jacobi.

Chapter 10

When she arrived at Rupert's apartment, her two companions were already waiting outside the building. Jacobi, his head still bandaged, stood under the awning of the entrance and Rupert was twenty yards away down the road. Holda got the distinct impression that neither of them had slept. Rupert could barely speak for yawning. Both were taciturn to the point of rudeness. She wondered whether they had argued and if so about what? However, her suggestion that they call by a local bakery to pick up croissants and coffee was unanimously accepted. Holda was also feeling the fact that she'd been up early and had missed her hotel breakfast.

With provisions safely on board, Holda turned the car in the direction of the Rhine. On the way she told the others about the impending arrival of Azriel and the fact that she had completed her transcription.

"I'll read it to you over breakfast at Father Jacobi's," she offered. "Assuming his house survived the night," she added, only half mischievously.

"I have a request for you Holda," announced Rupert. "There's a very old man I've been trying to get an appointment with to interview for a long time. He's aged one hundred and three, the oldest man in the town. He's been unwell in recent months and I haven't been able to speak with him. I got a phone call last night from one of his carers. She said he'd be willing to see me later this afternoon. I was wondering if you would be able to drive me over there. It's about eight kilometres. Only if your professor's visit doesn't get in the way, that is."

"I don't know," answered Holda cautiously. She felt even less trusting of Rupert this morning, though she couldn't explain why. "Let's see how Azriel wants to spend the day. Maybe he just wants to tuck himself up alone with the manuscript, in which case we needn't stay at the house the whole time."

Today might be a good day to start growing a beard, she thought wryly to herself. But surely Wilgefortis could have found some better way to remain a strong virgin than that?

"Somebody should keep an eye on the book though," pointed out Father Jacobi. "This professor chap of yours might not understand how perilous it is. I think perhaps I should stay with it."

"I think he already knows much more about its properties than any of us," answered Holda gravely. "But you're right. Between us we do need to keep an eye on the manuscript, and on Azriel."

She pulled the car up outside Father Jacobi's little house, which had indeed survived the night and was looking neat and squarely solid amid its rows of vegetables and herbs. Father Jacobi busied himself laying out plates, butter and jam in the kitchen to accompany their breakfast. Rupert ate little but slurped his coffee almost compulsively. Father Jacobi made him a second cup and Rupert's yawns began to subside. As soon as they had finished eating, Holda began to read out her translation of the last part of Johannes von Deibel's diary.

When she stopped, a shocked silence descended in the priests' kitchen.

"That is a horrible story," groaned Rupert at last. His voice was low and subdued and his face sagged with a combination of fatigue, disappointment and disgust. "We can't use those details in any public exhibition. The mayor will want something suitable for groups of schoolchildren. This book wouldn't even get an 18 plus rating if the censors got hold of it." He tried to force a laugh but it died in his throat.

Rupert is shocked, thought Holda. Even he stops being titillated once it goes beyond rape into the realm of Satanism, snuff porn and necrophilia. He really does look appalled. I wonder whether this is what Johannes von Deibel meant by the souls of the three of them haunting anyone who reads the book. Will we all wake up screaming every night out of petrifying nightmares, as these scenes play through our heads?

"Johannes von Deibel found a way to avoid the fires of Hell," breathed Father Jacobi as if to himself. "But which incantation was it that he used? There are so many in the book. I must read through it again." He stood up and moved towards the desk where the manuscript was lying. Holda turned and stared at him in alarm. In contrast to Rupert, his face was alert and resolute. Holda felt a wave of sudden fear run through her.

"No you don't, Father," she snapped shortly. "Don't touch it. Use the photos on my laptop. See if you can't find some way to reverse the spell and release poor Marieken and Wil Biskup."

She quickly placed herself between the priest and the book which was still lying open at the first of the blank pages. The words 'Kom mich ze helf' were still blackly visible at the top of the page.

"I would help you if I knew how, Marieken," she whispered.

At five minutes to one a taxi drew up outside Jacobi's house and a tall, gaunt figure in a black overcoat alighted. Professor Azriel Finster stepped through the garden gate and stood at the door of the house, his hand hovering over the doorbell. As he read the priest's name, which was printed on a small plastic plate under the bell, a curious expression crossed his features. Then he pressed the buzzer and listened to the priest's footsteps approaching down the hallway.

Holda was leafing through the Latin part of the manuscript at that moment in time and comparing it with Father Jacobi's handwritten notes. Rupert was behind her on the sofa making a list of questions he would like to ask of Meerbusch's oldest resident. As the doorbell rang, Holda stood up nervously and hovered half in the sitting room and half in the hall. She saw Jacobi open the front door and then take a step backwards, uttering a cry of alarm as he did so.

"Paulus Jacobi, we meet again," observed the professor. His voice sounded confident and amused. He gave a little chuckle. "They do say you always meet twice in a lifetime. But I should introduce myself. I go by the name of Azriel Finster now. Professor Finster if you don't mind. I gave up the name Ambrosius when I went into academia."

Jacobi was still gaping at the newcomer. His chest heaved up and down as though he were struggling to breathe.

Is he having a panic attack or is he in cardiac arrest, wondered Holda, but she stayed rooted to the spot like a rabbit watching a snake.

"I see you are still wearing a dog collar," went on Finster suavely, ignoring the evident distress of the older man. "I honestly don't know why you keep up the pretence. Or is it because it still means you get to spank the altar boys or stick your cock up their bottoms? Is it because the teenage girls come to you and whisper their dirty little secrets while you masturbate away in the confessional? I know what kind of a priest you used to be. In due course I shall tell you what I have become. But first I must see the manuscript."

He pushed past the priest and his gaze fixed on Holda who was clutching the living room doorframe.

"Ah, there you are, Holda," he barked. "Where is the book?"

"This way," answered Holda weakly. "It's in here on the desk," she added lamely as he pushed past her.

Rupert rose to his feet as Azriel entered the living room and stepped forward, his hand extended in greeting.

"I'm Rupert Keller. Very pleased to meet you," he began.

"Ah yes, Keller." Azriel ignored the outstretched palm but fixed Rupert with a superior glare. "Keller, the charming little Hitler who declined to send the book to Cambridge, occasioning me all the trouble and expense of dispatching Miss Weisel here." His gaze fell on his pupil. "Holda here must be the only student in Cambridge unable to connect her laptop to a Wi-Fi network and send an email. In the end, at great inconvenience to myself, I have come to Germany in person to get answers to my questions."

Rupert turned and retreated to the sofa, scowling.

"If I'd known the book caused whirlwinds and tried to murder people by dropping on them, I'd have been only too happy to post it to you," he muttered under his breath.

"I sent you my transcripts as soon as I could," protested Holda indignantly.

"I have read them on the journey," answered Azriel. "That part was well done I admit. But you failed to translate and interpret the astral calendar as I instructed. Fortunately, I was able to read that part myself from the photographs you sent. I had the dubious privilege of being taught Latin at a Jesuit seminary by none other than our own Paulus Jacobi, as he was then. A young priest of questionable character who used to teach Latin by day and sodomise the novices by night. If I suffer a prolapsed rectum later in life I shall know exactly whom to thank."

Jacobi's face appeared in the doorway. He looked grey and his forehead was beaded with sweat.

"Brother Ambrosius, I won't have you here in my house," he blustered.

"Paulus, you understand all about this manuscript and its significance for the two of us. You and I can both profit from this if we work together. But I warn you, if you turn me out of this house now, I will go straight to the police and have you arrested for the paedophile and rapist that you are. They will detain you for questioning for the next few days at least, during which time the planets will align. You know what that signifies."

Jacobi's mouth opened and closed several times, but no words emerged.

Azriel turned to Holda.

"Did Jacobi already try to have sex with you?"

Holda gasped. "No, of course not. How dare you... he wouldn't..."

Azriel chuckled in a way that was completely devoid of humour.

Holda felt her face burning and tears welling in her eyes.

How dare he speak like this? she thought fiercely. He's as vile as Johannes von Deibel. He wants me to be humiliated, making me transcribe that blasphemous, pornographic text. He's mocking me. Can those things he said about Jacobi be true though? It would tie in with him spying on couples making love on Gisela's bench. They are both horrible, wicked men. I will take Rupert to his interview this afternoon after all, just to get away from them.

"Come on Rupert," she called out furiously. "Let's leave them to it. They can study that damned book in peace. I'll drive you over to see your old man."

She snatched up her laptop, her bag and her parka and stormed out to the car where she sat, tears streaming down her face.

She wiped her eyes quickly when she saw Rupert coming out of the gate. His face was chalk white.

"Drive to Strümp, past Schloss Pesch and then turn right towards Ossum," he muttered quickly. The pitch of his voice wavered as he spoke, as though he were forcing the words through a constriction. "There's something I have to tell you on the way. We're still too early for our appointment with the old man at Haus Gripswald."

This had better not be a trick, thought Holda. After reading him that gruesome rape and murder story, who knows what's going through his head? A 'virgo fortis' must have an escape plan. I don't want to have to grow a beard. I need to rely on my own wits. For a start,

I must avoid stopping the car anywhere out of sight of inhabited settlements. I mustn't get myself into a position where I'm vulnerable to attack.

She set off, driving the route he had told her. Once they were out of view of the house, Rupert began to speak.

"It's all true, what your professor says about Jacobi," he blurted out. "I was in his choir and his confirmation classes. When I was seven, I broke a window in the church one day by accident. He made me stay behind after choir practice as punishment. He took me into the vestry where the broken window was and made me kneel on a chair. I remember he locked the door behind him. Then he pulled down my shorts and pants and pulled a gym shoe out of his bag. He told me to repeat the lord's prayer, but reversing the order of the lines starting with 'For ever and ever, amen.' At the end of every line he whacked me hard on the buttocks with the gym shoe. Every time I got it wrong he made me start all over again, until I was crying so hard I couldn't remember any of the words at all. I don't know how long it went on. It felt like hours and my bottom hurt horribly. Finally I managed to complete the prayer in reverse. Then he made me get off the chair and bend over with my hands on the seat."

Rupert's voice sank to a hoarse whisper.

"Then he told me that if you say the lord's prayer backwards you will go straight to Hell. The only thing that could save my soul would be if he planted his seeds in me. And then he pulled down his trousers and buggered me."

"Oh Rupert," whispered Holda, risking a sympathetic glance at him as they pulled up to a red light.

"That's horrible. You were so young too. I don't know what to say."

The light changed to green and they drove on.

"That man ruined my whole life," went on Rupert bitterly. "He told me it was all my fault and that I was wicked. Lots of things like that. I believed him, of course. He said that I was gay and if I ever told any person the whole town would find out. That was a big stigma back then, especially when I was only seven. I was terrified that people would be able to tell what had happened just by looking at me."

Rupert took a couple of deep breaths and then carried on, his voice still unsteady.

"For the next two years, until I was nine, he sodomised me regularly. He called it cleansing me. It was horrible and I felt ashamed and guilty. Then one day my mother saw blood in my pants and asked me about it. I denied everything but she had her suspicions. We started going to a different church after that. As soon as I was able to I stopped going to church at all. But that Catholic guilt never leaves you. All through my teens I believed I was homosexual. In reality, I wasn't even attracted to other men. I was afraid of them after what had happened. I stayed away from women too and never had a girlfriend because I thought no girl could ever like me after that. You are the only person I've ever told. I thought I was the only one he did it to. I only found out today, from your professor, that there were other victims."

They were passing by the graveyard in Strümp. Holda pulled the car into the car park there, stopped in the first bay and looked across at Rupert. His face was now blurred by the tears welling in her own eyes.

She wiped them quickly and then reached across and brushed away the wet streaks on Rupert's cheeks. The kindliness of her touch caused him to break into uncontrollable sobs and Holda spontaneously shed more tears of sympathy. At that moment they seemed like two desolate children sitting side by side sharing nothing but a common miserable loneliness.

Holda was the first to speak.

"You look like a man who could use a hug," she consoled him, and then started at her own words. Holda had never uttered anything like that to anyone in her life before. Come to think of it, she wasn't sure she had even hugged anyone previously. Did she even know how?

Just do it, she told herself sternly. She undid her seatbelt, leaned over and put her arms awkwardly around Rupert's neck. She could feel the sobs juddering through his whole body, a tide of grief which she was powerless to stem.

I can't make this right, thought Holda in alarm, I don't know how to help him. But then, instinctively, she realised that she did know.

She continued to hold him, her arms squeezing him with just enough pressure to be reassuring but without damaging his injured shoulder. Her brain grappled for suitable words but found none, so she remained silent. Her stillness gradually seemed to communicate itself to Rupert. The shaking subsided and his breathing steadied.

After what seemed like an age he pulled away and smiled at her, his blue eyes still wet with tears, but his face now radiating relief and gratitude. Holda surprised herself by leaning in and kissing him. His one good arm pulled her to him and suddenly their tongues were touching, probing, exploring one another.

How long they stayed locked in their first kiss neither Holda nor Rupert could say afterwards. Eventually Rupert pulled away and murmured, "I could stay like this with you forever. But we do need to be at Haus Gripswald to see the old gentleman in five minutes. It's really not far from here. We'll still make it if we leave now."

"I'd rather stay here with you too," replied Holda and with a shock she realised that she really meant it. Was it Rupert's confession that had changed her feelings towards him so dramatically? Or was it the seven kilometre distance that now lay between them and the manuscript?

I don't know what to think any more, thought Holda anxiously. I feel so attracted to Rupert, but what if my initial instinct was right and he's actually dangerous? I felt sorry for him when he told me about his childhood, but perhaps I'm just sympathetic because I was also lonely and bullied when I was young. Kissing him felt so wonderful though. Which instinct is the right one?

"I wish we could drive off and never go back to that ghastly manuscript and those two awful men," she blurted out. "Can you imagine that, Rupert? If we could just walk away from the whole thing?" She sighed resignedly. "But duty calls. We'd better get going to your interview."

Holda turned on the engine and put the car into gear.

"Who is this old gentleman anyway?" she enquired as they pulled out onto the road. "Can I come in with you, or will I be in the way?"

"Of course you can come in and see him," answered Rupert. His voice had almost returned to normal now.

"Turn right here. The house is hidden in those trees at the end of this track."

Holda pulled the car into a narrow, unpaved roadway and realised it was exactly the kind of location she'd resolved to avoid. For reasons she couldn't explain, she no longer felt apprehensive.

"He's also a Catholic priest," continued Rupert, "but he preceded Papa Jacobi. He was retired before I was even born. He lives in an old, fortified manor house on the edge of the forest. It's used nowadays as a retirement retreat for clergy. There are about five elderly nuns looking after all the old priests." He smiled wryly. "A bargain arrangement for the church. I wonder whether the isolation is worse for the clergy or for the nuns."

They pulled up to a huge, old, brick fortress built around a courtyard with a vast circular turret on one corner.

"When it was constructed it had a moat around it but that was filled in sometime in the seventeenth century," explained Rupert. "The turret is the oldest part of the building. The onion dome was added in the eighteen century when another storey was added. The base of the tower is thought to be medieval."

The eternal archivist, thought Holda indulgently to herself. He always needs to know the story behind people and places.

"I had been wondering yesterday," added Rupert, "whether this might not have been the tower Johannes von Deibel lived in. The location must be more or less right."

Holda shuddered involuntarily. Would she never be free from that awful manuscript?

"I don't want to think about von Deibel or the book," she retorted crossly. "Let's go and see the old priest and hope he has some pleasant reminiscences for us."

As they entered through an archway into a huge, cobbled courtyard, a middle-aged nun in a grey habit strode briskly towards them. She had that no-nonsense air which reminded Holda of a matron in a military hospital.

"You must be Rupert Keller," she declared curtly. "I'm Sister Barbara. Father Dietrich is expecting you."

Rupert introduced Holda and the nun led them through a doorway at the base of the tower, and up a winding staircase to a bright room on the first floor. In an armchair by the window was the hunched, sticklike figure of a very ancient man. The few strands of hair on his head were pure white. His face was lined all over like crumpled tissue paper. His eye sockets were so deep and his lids so saggy that he barely seemed to possess any eyeballs. His head lolled on his chest as though it would be too much effort to hold it up. He was dressed in a priest's garb and had a woollen blanket tucked around his legs. Holda could see the edge of a urine bag sticking out from the cover.

"Father Dietrich," called the nun in that strident voice that members of the nursing profession often reserve for the elderly, "your visitors are here. Rupert Keller and a Miss Weisel."

Chapter 11

The old man inched his head upwards as though it pained him and forced the drooping eyelids open a fraction. There was a wheezing sound from his chest, and then words creaked from his dry, old lips.

"Thank you Sister Barbara. Please friends, be seated."

His voice scraped as though he had not used it for a very long time.

Rupert and Holda pulled up two armchairs facing each other, one on either side of the old man, whose chair faced the window. Sister Barbara bustled out of the room, shutting the door behind her.

"Thank you for inviting me," began Rupert. "I really appreciate that you could find time to talk. I hope you don't mind, but I brought Miss Weisel along too. She will take notes as needed. I'm a bit out of action I'm afraid." He indicated his arm tucked in the sling.

The old head cranked itself round to face him.

"There is no time for pleasantries, my son," rasped the old priest. "I am one hundred and three years old and fading. I probably only have a few days left, possibly only a few hours. There is something I urgently need to share with you. It may be of vital importance."

Rupert raised his eyebrows and cast a glance over to Holda. She looked equally puzzled but leaned forward, silently encouraging the old man to continue.

"I have heard about you going around the villages gathering tittle tattle and tales of nostalgic nonsense," went on the priest to Rupert, his chest wheezing like an old pair of bellows. "Use your position wisely, young man. Remember that some stories are best left untold. Other news needs to be shouted from the church steeple. Yours is a task that requires wisdom and judgement. All stories are not the same."

He broke off again, as though the effort of speaking was too great for him.

"I will do my best, Father," replied Rupert, filling the silence while the old man caught his breath.

"I know the truth behind all the stories," hissed the old man. "I was Father Confessor here to the population for over thirty years. I know what went on. These are the stories that I must leave untold, for they are not mine to tell. The secrecy of the confessional must never be broken."

His hooded eyes were fixed now on the middle distance. He seemed to be speaking to the treetops outside the window rather than to Rupert and Holda.

"In all my years as a priest I have listened to all the sins. Always the same sins over and over: envy, spite, greed, fornication, adultery, violence, rape. Always I listened, prayed, assigned penances and offered the lord's forgiveness. Only twice in my time have I withheld the absolution. Twice there were such terrible crimes that not even God could forgive. Of one of those cases we shall not speak, for the person concerned is still living and his soul is already lost to the lord. It is about the other that I wished to see you."

Another pause. This time the priest seemed to be searching in his brain for the right words. His breathing seemed to have eased a little.

"In the case of the other man, I refused for sixty years to hear his confession. His crime I already knew about. Everyone has heard about it yet nobody speaks of it. There is no doubt in my mind that his soul is lost. And yet..." Again the old man's voice tailed off.

"I am old, my children," he resumed at last. "When I passed ninety my health began to fail, though mercifully not my mind. I have not left this room now for thirteen years. I sit here waiting for blessed death to come for me, but it stays away. Why?" The old head swivelled alarmingly as he glared fiercely, first at Rupert and then at Holda, from his sunken, pinprick eyes.

"Why does death not come? It can only be because God still has some purpose in keeping me alive. I must still achieve something before I am permitted to leave this life. But what could it be? I am a hundred and three and can do nothing for myself anymore."

He wheezed again and this time the mucous seemed to shift a little and his voice continued, stronger than before.

"I prayed for enlightenment and then I remembered one thing that might be considered unfinished business. It was a letter which was given to me over sixty years ago by one of my parishioners on his deathbed. That letter had been passed to him by an aunt, who had it from her mother, who in turn had inherited it from her grandfather's sister. The letter had been written to that lady from her fiancé, an upright and godly man who had vanished one night suddenly and unexpectedly. She was convinced he must have been caught up in some terrible accident, as it would have been out of character for him to leave without warning. The letter contained his confession to such a crime as has, thank God, never been seen in these parts since. A crime so hideous that no absolution for it could ever be possible. He begged her to take the letter to the parish priest and ask him to read it. He pleaded for the priest to pray for him and intercede on his behalf. But the good lady was so horrified by what she read that she hid the confession and did not show it to anyone. After her death, the descendants who inherited the document in turn all chose to hide it away. My parishioner was the last of his line and he entrusted it to me."

"And what did the letter say?" asked Holda breathlessly.

The old head swung to observe her.

"I did not read it," answered the priest after a moment's silence. "My parishioner told me of its contents and I did not wish to read such a wicked document. Besides, the man who wrote it must have long since met his maker and answered for his crimes. What good could I do? Or so I thought at the time. But now, as God continues to withhold the blessing of death from me, I begin to wonder. I was the first priest to be handed this confession. Could it be that the author's soul is still in limbo after all these years, awaiting my intercession?"

"So have you read the confession now?" asked Rupert eagerly.

"I have not. I cannot. My eyes are too weak. But even if that were not the case, the letter is written in the old, florid, gothic handwriting of the early nineteenth century. I cannot make out the words. That is why I asked you to come here. As an archivist, I take it you can read old documents?"

"I can certainly give it a try," offered Rupert. "When I trained as a librarian we had to deal with a lot of old manuscripts. You'd be surprised how many of our ancestors had appalling handwriting."

The old man hoisted his head again and looked severely at Rupert. His already withered face was folded now into even deeper lines.

"You will know some of the details already. The author of this letter was Heinrich Plenkers and in it he confesses to the gruesome murder of Henrietta von Hüls, and the man whose body was found alongside hers. It won't make for pleasant reading."

Holda exhaled slowly and caught Rupert's eye. His blue orbs were alive with emotion, mirroring her own.

"I'd be honoured to try to read it for you, if you'll allow it," he announced solemnly, trying his best to conceal his rising excitement.

"You will find the document in the top left hand drawer of the cabinet behind you," went on the priest. "Bring it over here to the light and see whether you can decipher it."

Rupert stood up, walked over to the cabinet indicated and returned holding a yellowish folded document with a broken red seal on one side. On the front was an address written in exaggeratedly sloping handwriting in faded brown ink. The capital letters and those with stalks were each written with a strong flourish, but the small characters all looked very uniform.

It's hard to distinguish them from one another, thought Holda.

Rupert sat down again and was about to unfold the letter when the priest extended a scrawny claw and grasped his good hand.

"Before you read it," he urged, "remember that this is a man's confession of his sins. He did not write it for the entertainment of future generations, this is a man wrestling with the devil for his own soul. Whatever you may think of Heinrich Plenkers after you have heard his story, you must keep his secret. Do I have your word on this?"

"Yes. Of course. I understand completely," replied Rupert, looking crestfallen. Holda nodded silent acquiescence.

The priest leaned back in his chair. His eyes disappeared back into their hollows.

"You may begin."

Rupert unfolded the stiff yellowing pages, smoothed them out on his lap and began to read the first page:

My dearest, darling Lisette,

You must be frantic with worry after I left Strümp so suddenly one month ago without saying goodbye. Alas, I cannot allay any of your fears for I remain in mortal peril. I fear I am lost to you forever. I have seen and heard things which no man should ever experience. I have committed a crime for which my soul shall surely pay a terrible price. Yet I still cling to a shred of hope that our dear lord will show me mercy. Though the crime I committed was a mortal sin, I truly believe that by my act, I prevented the downfall of all mankind.

The old priest heaved himself upright in his armchair and, with a shaking hand, crossed himself.

I have enclosed here my account of everything that occurred on the night of April 30th. I can still scarcely give it credence myself, darling Lisette, but believe me every word of it really is true. I have composed my story in the form of a written confession. I ask you to place this document in the hands of Father Adam and beg him to pray for intercession on my behalf.

I am writing to you from Marseille and I sail tonight for Alexandria. I must spend my remaining life in exile, for if I am found I will surely be hanged. In the Orient I shall not find any Christian father confessor, so Father Adam's intercession may be the only chance to save my soul.

Believe me darling, not a day, not an hour passes when you are not in my mind and heart. Your name is the first word on my lips when I wake and the last thing I utter before I sleep. Your absence in my life is as dire a torture to me as any that Satan may be preparing for me. I can, however, never return to the Rhineland. It grieves me more than words can tell to write this, but I release you from our betrothal. There, my heart is broken at these words and even now my tears splash onto the page and I have smudged my writing. You are free my darling. Live your life in peace and do as God wills. I pray that you will remember me fondly.

I remain, dearest Lisette, your obedient servant,
Heinrich Plenkers

Rupert put down the first page and picked up the second.

"This part is the confession," he declared, as he scanned it. The old priest crossed himself again. His head remained upright, the tiny specks of his eyes watched Rupert carefully as he read:

Please bless me Father, for I have sinned. My last confession was over five weeks ago at our beautiful chapel in Ossum. Since then my life has turned upside down and I find myself a murderer in exile, and in mortal peril for my soul. But wait, I must first explain exactly what happened and confess my sins. Forgive me, I am in such turmoil, I can scarcely think straight.

It started on April 30th just before dawn. I was up around five as usual to milk the cows on the rear meadow. It was just getting light as I led the cattle back down to pasture from the milking shed, and there was a light mist about. Suddenly, in the grey light I saw the ghost. It was down where the ruins of the burned out old house stand. It was a tall figure in a dark grey coat with tails, white breeches, a blue cravat, a black high hat and black riding boots. He was standing with his back to me but I recognised him at once as Lady Henrietta's Dutch visitor, the scholar from Utrecht, who died in the fire thirteen years ago and was so badly burned that his body was never found. As I stared he turned around and I saw that his ghastly spectral face was badly disfigured from the fire, or maybe from decay, for I am certain he was already long dead. Part of his upper lip was missing and his upper teeth and gums were showing in a way that still makes me shudder to recollect.

I took to my heels and ran back to the house where I told Elise and Anke in the dairy what I had seen. We all crossed ourselves and said the lord's prayer, and then went back to our day's work.

Later in the morning, Lady Henrietta came down to the stables where I was grooming the carriage horses and asked me to carry a wooden crate from her drawing room, on the first floor of the new schloss, down to her little private chapel to the left of the main building.

She told me I was to leave it in front of the altar and under no circumstances was I to open it or look inside. It was a very heavy box and I noticed there was a strange, unpleasant smell about it. As I was coming out of the main doorway, I thought I caught sight of the same figure in the grey frockcoat and high hat ducking behind the trees on the other side of the chapel. I couldn't investigate while I was carrying that heavy crate, and by the time I'd taken it to where her ladyship wanted it and come out again, there was nobody there. It did make me wonder though, whether it had been a ghost or was really an intruder.

I saw Lady Henrietta again as I left the chapel and she told me to come up to her boudoir as there was something else to be brought down. She led the way up there. I told her about the ghost I had seen that morning. I don't know why but that put her in high spirits, and she laughed heartily as though it were the greatest of jests. In her boudoir there was an old book lying on her writing table, and she pointed at it and told me to carry it very carefully to the chapel and lay it on the altar. I looked at the volume and, I do not know why, I felt a great reluctance to touch it and I told her so. At this she flew into a rage and declared the book was the most marvellous tome in the world and that if she would only write her name in it using her own blood, she could never again fall into the hands of Satan or be punished by God. She acted so strangely that I was more afraid of her than of that old book. I picked it up and carried it to the chapel as she had commanded. Then I went back to my work and was careful to stay out of her ladyship's way for the rest of the day.

After the evening milking, I stepped out to Lisette's house as usual and we walked for a while in the woods.

We did kiss each other frequently Father, but I strove to keep my thoughts as pure as a man can under the circumstances. We planned we would speak to you the following Sunday to ask you for a date in June for our wedding. I returned to the schloss very late; long after nightfall.

As I walked through the side gate I happened to look across the grand driveway towards the corner where the chapel stands. To my surprise I saw dim lights moving about inside that building. I decided to take a look inside as I feared someone might be trying to steal the chapel silver. I hastened over there and peered through the big, arched window by the doorway.

I could just make out a figure moving about, setting lighted candles on the altar and apparently making other preparations for Mass. Then I heard a noise from over by the schloss. I quickly hid myself in the shadows and watched. I saw her ladyship come out of the main door of the house, as naked as the day she was born, and make her way towards where I was concealed in a niche in the chapel wall. I held my breath in fright as she went by, so afraid was I that she might see me.

She entered the chapel and I could hear her speaking with someone there. It was a male voice with a guttural accent that answered her, but I did not catch the words for they spoke in low tones. I crept back to the window but I could see nothing in the interior of the chapel, for it was lit by only two stinking tapers.

What happened next is a terrifying mystery to me. I shall do my best to describe what I heard and saw and hope it makes more sense to you, Father, than it did to me.

The man's voice rose and he declaimed some words in a language which might have been Latin, Greek or

Arabic. I am not familiar with any of those languages for, as you know, we in this part of the country speak only Rhineland Dutch at church and at home. Shortly after there followed a sound like thunder and another voice started to speak. This was a loud booming voice, the deepest voice I ever heard. It was not shouting, it was more like a thunderous growling whisper, but it half deafened me all the same. This voice I could comprehend though, dear God, I wish I had not understood it.

'You have summoned me,' the voice uttered, 'yet I see no young virgin restrained in straps of man-leather and spread on the altar for me to penetrate. What treachery is this?'

Then I heard her ladyship's voice say, 'I am the virgin you seek. I eagerly await Your Majesty's pleasure. See, I place myself upon the altar in anticipation of receiving your black seed. Together we shall conceive the one true almighty anti-Christ who will reap the souls of all mankind and give you, my lord, victory for all eternity over God and his false angels. I myself shall triumph over the feeble virgin Mary who begat only a sap to be tortured and killed by his enemies.'

As you can imagine, I listened to these wicked words with terror in my heart. But nothing could have prepared me for what I heard next. There was a sound like a snarling beast and then her ladyship began to cry out. Her first words were, 'Take me, oh my master.' Then she screamed louder and cried out, 'I am torn asunder, have mercy, I beseech you!'

The grunting and growling carried on though and my lady's howls grew louder and more piteous. I dared not move or assist her. I knew by then that Satan himself was in that accursed chapel and I was powerless to intervene.

Then my ladyship gave a terrifying shriek which ended in a sort of gurgle. The snarling died away to a sort of savage chomping sound and then a vile stench filled the air. I heard the guttural male voice speak. My ladyship was howling wordlessly like a wounded animal.

At this point I summoned all my courage and crept around to the chapel door. It was slightly ajar and I peeped inside. My ladyship was lying naked across the altar howling. Strange markings were daubed on her flesh and on the floor. From between her thighs was dripping blood mixed with a black viscous liquid. Where her mouth should have been there was just a red bubbling hole from which a wordless, bellowing noise emerged. Standing over her was the ghost I had seen that morning, the spectre of the Dutch scholar with the burnt face.

Without thinking what I was doing, I picked up a rock from the ground near the chapel doorway and ran into the chapel, smiting at the ghostly head with it. My rock hit firm flesh. The ghost was a solid man, though his face was badly disfigured by burning. He stumbled under the blow. I hit him again and he fell down on his back. In a frenzy I smashed the rock into his face repeatedly, until he lay still, his face a mask of bloody flesh like my ladyship's.

All this time Lady Henrietta was still alive. But I knew that she had already been impregnated with the spawn of Satan himself. If she lived, the anti-Christ would be born among us and every soul on Earth would be in peril.

I had my hunting knife on my belt. I pulled it out and cut her throat, there where she lay. As the blood poured from her neck, her body convulsed and soon she was still. Then, as she lay dead before me, I completely severed her head from her neck, just to be sure. Next to the altar on the floor lay that accursed book of hers. I would have borne it away from there and destroyed it, but I could not bear to carry it with me. There was a lead box by the altar containing a few strange, tallow lights. I threw out those candles and put the book into the box. Then I hid it in a niche near the altar, one that was intended to be used for keeping the sacraments. There were still some bricks and tools lying at the back of the chapel, for the building had only been completed recently. I bricked up that niche so that the vile book might never be found. I sealed the niche with symbols to ward off evil so that the devil might not find it, and so that the villainous text might not escape from its hiding place. It must be something supremely malevolent from what Lady Henrietta had said about writing her name in it in blood and then being beyond the reach of God or Satan. When I remembered her words, I did one more terrible thing. I went to my lady's corpse and, with my knife, I cut off her right hand. I hid it in the pocket of my coat. After that I fetched the grey mare from the stables, rode her direct to the river and threw the dead hand into the fast flowing Rhine. They do say that the devil cannot abide flowing water and I wanted to ensure no demon could return my ladyship's hand for to her to sign her name with.

After that I fled the scene. I knew my life would be forfeit if I were found. I rode southeast avoiding towns and villages lest my route should be tracked. By dawn

I was well on the way to Aachen and from there I travelled to Brussels, Paris and now down through France to the coast.

I have committed additional sins on my journey for I have stolen both food and money to further my escape. I cannot risk stopping and working for my living, for the news of Lady Henrietta's death will surely follow me swiftly and I will be recognised.

For these sins too, I ask forgiveness. But nothing I have done can imperil my soul as does the murder and defilement of the corpse of my Lady Henrietta. Please God, I repent of these sins and any others which I have failed to mention, and by the help of your grace I shall endeavour not to sin again.

Heinrich Plenkers

Chapter 12

As Rupert finished speaking, he and Holda both looked across at the old priest. For a moment, Holda wondered whether he was still breathing as he was sitting so still. His eyelids closed and there was the laboured sound of a deep intake of breath. Then his eyes flicked open wider than Holda had yet seen them and he spoke, his voice clear and strong.

"Dominus noster Jesus Christus te absolvat; et ego auctoritate ipsius te absolvo ab omni vinculo excommunicationis et interdicti in quantum possum et tu indiges. Deinde, ego te absolvo a peccatis tuis in nomine Patris, et Filii, et et Spiritus Sancti. Amen."

As he spoke he made the sign of the cross.

"The absolution," mouthed Rupert to Holda.

He's forgotten I speak Latin, thought Holda, but she nodded acknowledgement all the same.

It was a long time before anyone spoke. Then the priest's face scrunched together and he queried slowly, "That book. I heard that a book had been found in the chapel at Schloss Pesch recently."

"Yes, Father, that's the one," answered Rupert tensely. "The manuscript was found exactly where Heinrich Plenkers says he hid it. That book is a horrible diary written by a devil worshipper called Johannes von Deibel in 1361. It contains spells and other diabolical writings and explains how to raise the devil. It's like a handbook for raising the anti-Christ."

"What did she mean about signing her name in blood and being safe from God and the devil?" demanded the old man sharply.

Rupert gulped and looked across at Holda.

"Father," blurted out Holda, reaching across and grasping the old man's hand, "the book is bound in the skin of a man who was hanged and some of the pages are made from the skin of a girl who was raped and murdered. Part of the diary is written using Johannes von Deibel's blood as ink. He says that by using their skin and his blood, and by his black magic, their souls are trapped in the book for all eternity. I believe it because on a page made from the skin of the girl, some writing appears in medieval German pleading for help."

The old priest's eyes darted sharply from one to the other, as though he were testing whether they were serious.

"I swear it's true, Father," cried Holda, and felt as though she wanted to burst into tears. "Her name is Marieken and she needs us to find a way to release her. Her friend Wil is trapped too. That book is evil and corrupt. Terrible things happen around it. The tornado that struck Lank-Latum the other day destroyed the building where it was kept."

"Where is the volume now?" demanded Father Dietrich fiercely.

"It is at Father Jacobi's house," answered Rupert.

"Jacobi? Paulus Jacobi?" The old priest's voice had risen to a shrill screech and he half rose to his feet, before sinking defeated back into his armchair, his body crumpling into a wheezy coughing fit. It was several minutes before he could speak again.

"God has started to reveal to me his purpose in keeping me alive so long," he announced when his power of speech had returned. "When you came here, I mentioned there were only ever two confessions for which I had not granted absolution. One was an omission of my own which I have rectified just now. The other I dare not describe without breaching the sanctity of the confessional...and yet..." His voice wavered. "And yet now I learn that that one remaining damned soul who wilfully and willingly turned his back on God, is now in possession of this devil's missal. Why has this revelation come to me only now, when I am too old to act? How can it be that that wicked villain has in his hands the means to escape God's wrath and the pits of Hell? Why are the tools to destroy all mankind placed in his of all hands?"

"Not just his," cried Holda with rising panic in her voice, "Azriel is with him too."

"Holda is the academic who deciphered the text," explained Rupert in response to Father Dietrich's bewildered look. "Azriel Finster is her university professor. Let's just say that he also seems to be unnaturally interested in the contents of this manuscript."

"Do you know the manner by which the fiend is summoned from the pits of Hell?" demanded Father Dietrich. "We need to know what they are planning to do, in order to prevent it."

Holda fished in her bag and pulled out her notebook.

"I can read you what Johannes von Deibel says," she offered. "Hold onto your blanket though Father; it's a terrifying and lewd story."

"I'll have heard worse in the confessional," he answered grimly.

"I'd be very surprised if you have, Father," muttered Rupert.

As Holda read her translation of the diary aloud, the old priest gripped the arms of his chair with his gnarled fingers. At certain parts of the tale his face slackened to an expression of horror, at others it crumpled to a fierce scowl.

When she had finished, the old priest spoke.

"I believe there may be a way to release the souls of Marieken and Wil and destroy the manuscript for ever. Are you able to get possession of the book again?"

"I should say so," asserted Rupert. "It belongs to my archive. It's up to me where the book is kept. Though finding a suitable place to keep it hasn't been easy."

The priest looked at him sharply.

"The book doesn't need to be kept safe," Father Dietrich growled. "It is mankind that needs to be protected from danger. For that to happen, the manuscript must be destroyed."

"But what about Marieken and Wil?" cried Holda.

"You must do the following. You need to unbind the manuscript. You must literally take it apart. You must unstitch and unglue the binding and separate the covering and the pages which are made from Marieken and Wil from the wicked writing which channels the powers of Satan and his demons. You must bring me all those pieces in three separate packages, carefully labelled. Over Marieken and Wil I will say the absolution of the dead followed by a Requiem Mass. When I die, which can surely not be long now, these two packets will be placed in my coffin with me and buried with all proper liturgies in the hallowed churchyard at Strümp. If God wills it, their souls shall accompany me to the last judgement and, if it is in my power, I will intercede on their behalf. The third parcel we will cremate together here in the fireplace. If I am correct, that fire will release Johannes von Deibel's soul to a still hotter inferno, which is where it belongs for the rest of eternity."

"Right," cried Rupert jumping to his feet, "we need to get that manuscript."

"Take great care," cautioned the priest. "Jacobi and your professor will not give up the document without a struggle. If I were young I would go in your place, but God has willed it otherwise. Before you go, allow me to bless you both, that the lord may keep you safe from the forces of evil."

Holda and Rupert both knelt in front of the old man's armchair while he placed a hand on each of their heads and pronounced a Latin blessing over them.

"Now go in God's name and may you succeed in your quest," he urged. "Godspeed, my children."

With that, Holda and Rupert rose, spoke their thanks and goodbyes, descended the staircase, waved across the courtyard to Sister Barbara and hurried back to Holda's car.

As she started up the engine, Holda appealed, "We need to think, Rupert. We must have a plan. Before we rush into Jacobi's house and try to get the book away from them we need to think about how best to do it."

"Let's drive over to the Rhine," suggested Rupert. "It's a beautiful afternoon. We'll find somewhere quiet and plot our strategy."

Holda pointed the vehicle east and they drove the two kilometres along a country road which snaked towards the vast, grey river.

Father Dietrich was right when he described it as a quest, thought Holda. This is the part where we have to fight the dragons and save the damsel in distress. This is where I need all the cunning and resourcefulness of Wilgefortis and the help of the holy virgin.

Holda slammed on the brakes suddenly.

"The virgin!" she exclaimed.

"What's up?" asked Rupert alarmed. "Why on earth did you stop like that? What virgin?"

"I read it in your legends book," retorted Holda. "You left it in my car the other night. It was on the first page. The miracle of Wilgefortis."

"The bearded lady?" asked Rupert. "What has that story got to do with anything?"

Holda pushed the car into gear again and drove off more quickly.

"The name Wilgefortis comes from virgo fortis. It means strong virgin in Latin. But that's the whole point. She isn't strong. A crowd of men are chasing her and about to rape her. She's vulnerable. But she's also brave and cunning. She comes to a wayside cross and she jumps up and stretches her arms. She gets some extra help from the virgin Mary who sends her facial hair as a disguise, but basically Wilgefortis outwits her enemies with fancy footwork and a sharp mind."

"I still don't get it," grumbled Rupert as they pulled into the car park by the Rhine.

"Don't you see?" Holda yelled urgently across the car roof at Rupert's emerging figure. "Azriel's come to see the book because of the planetary alignment which will be sometime in the next hours or days. He's there in that house right now, reading up on how to raise the devil. He's learning the incantations and finding out what he needs. He may even have sent Jacobi out to murder some infants for candles, for all we know."

Rupert stared at her with open mouthed realisation on his face.

"Exactly," she shouted, trying to hold down her panic. "The virgin. They have to have a virgin. That must be me."

"Get back into the car," yelled Rupert urgently. "We'll drive to the airport. I'll put you on a plane to...to anywhere far away."

"No. You've got your arm in a sling and we still have to get that book away from them. It has to be destroyed. Marieken has to be saved. If I'm not around, they'll just kidnap a different virgin from somewhere. Jacobi knows exactly who has and hasn't had sex yet because he spies on them and he hears their confessions. Between the two of them they'll just find a replacement. Rupert, they have to think their virgin's me until it's too late for them to get a substitute."

"But it's much too dangerous!" protested Rupert.

"For me or for the rest of the world?" hissed Holda fiercely. "I am one person. Let's look at the big picture."

"For me, Holda, you are the big picture," groaned Rupert helplessly, his blue eyes brimming up. "Holda, I love you. I'd die if something happened to you."

Holda stared at him for a moment with an expression of astonishment on her features. Then she exclaimed, "Rupert, you're a genius! That's the answer. Don't you see?"

"Right now I don't see anything," pleaded Rupert helplessly. "I only see a beautiful, crazy girl who won't see sense and save herself."

"Oh yes I will," countered Holda briskly. "Rupert. We need to have sex right now, this minute. Don't you understand? I'm only valuable to them as long as I'm a virgin. Once I'm no longer pure, I'm not a suitable vessel for Satan's seed. But Jacobi and Azriel won't suspect I've changed. They won't think to look for a stand-in. Whatever happens to me, at least we won't bring the anti-Christ down on the world."

Rupert looked at her in bewilderment. "Are you saying you want to have sex? With me? What I mean is, it's a nice idea and all that," he added in obvious embarrassment, "but are you sure that's how it works? Won't the devil just rape you in revenge, or do something even worse? Oh God, remember that bit about ripping tongues out!"

"We have to try it," insisted Holda. "Come on Rupert, please."

"What, here? Are you mad? You want us to have sex now, in a car park?"

"No. There's a secret place just the other side of the dyke, right down by the river. It's like a little sandy cove, sheltered by steep banks. Come on, we'll be there in two minutes. Follow me."

"How do you know this?" asked Rupert.

"That's something I should have told you before, Rupert. I lived in Ossum a long time ago when I was a little girl. I used to come down here on my own and play when I was seven or eight. It was one of my secret places. Come on, I'll show you."

She grabbed Rupert's good hand, led the way through the trees, and helped him down a steep path to the sandy shore by the side of the Rhine. From there they followed the shore downstream for a few minutes until they reached a place where two promontories jutted out towards the water's edge. Between them was a little sandy cove, sheltered from view from the land side.

"When the river is higher, it's hard to reach," explained Holda. "But today it's easy enough. We can't be seen, except perhaps from a distance by people on passing barges."

"Holda, I told you I love you," began Rupert, "but I really don't know whether we should do this. It all seems so sudden. What I mean to say is, are you just trying to lose your virginity any way you can? Or do you actually...like me?"

Holda turned her large, green eyes on him and moved her face closer to his. "Of course I do," she breathed. "Rupert, I love you more than I've ever loved anyone in my life."

"You are one amazing woman," whispered Rupert. He put his good arm around her shoulders and pulled her in for a long and ardent kiss.

How strange it is, thought Holda, as she relished the sensation of his warm tongue pushing into her mouth, that I'm not even nervous. Maybe it's because he has one arm out of action. I might be frightened of a man who I thought could overpower me. But with Rupert injured, I'd always be able to get away. But I don't even want to escape. His physical closeness is exciting and somehow comforting. I really do want this. When I told him I loved him just now, perhaps I was right. Maybe I really am starting to love him. I wonder if this is what falling in love feels like.

As this barrage of thoughts streamed through her mind, a thrill started at her lips and ran down to her crotch, which tingled hotly inside her jeans. The sensation was unfamiliar and strangely thrilling. She instinctively drew Rupert closer. Rupert's good hand was sliding down her body now, pausing to caress her breasts then working its way lower to cup her buttocks and pull her hips against him.

Everywhere he touches me it feels like an electric current is flowing, Holda thought. It's like we're creating some kind of amazing, beautiful magic between us.

She reached down, unbuttoned Rupert's jeans, then lowered his zip.

I can't believe I'm really doing this, she thought. But I'm in control. It's my choice. The strong virgin is choosing not to be a virgin any more. Facial hair not required.

Holda pulled away and took off her parka, laying it on the dry part of the sand between the strongly flowing Rhine and the steep upward slope of the river bank, veined with the roots of the overhanging trees.

"Let's do it here," she whispered in his ear. "This can be our bed. Let's make it special."

"It's my first time too," murmured Rupert back. "You can't count what Jacobi did. Let's deflower each other." They kissed again with the violent energy that only flows between two lovers who are abandoning all control to passion. Holda helped Rupert pull off his clothes, stripped off her own garments and they sank naked together onto the sandy bed.

"You'll have to be on top," whispered Rupert. "I can't put weight on my arm."

He lay flat while Holda straddled him. As she pressed the lips of her vagina onto his erection, applying her weight cautiously at first, she felt her body resist for a moment and then yield. Rupert was inside her. She could sense his penis pulsating inside her body. She began to move her hips to the rhythm of the throbbing in her loins and at the same time she threw back her head and let out a great shout of unbridled joy.

They completely lost track of time down there at the riverbank. The newness of their glorious relationship, their own need for physical and emotional closeness, even the sheer excitement of being naked in the open air intoxicated them and made them reckless. In between lovemaking they lay in each other's arms, alternating between talking excitedly and hugging one another silently. They caressed and savoured each other's smooth, warm skin. Holda was the adventurous one. She pushed for trying as many positions as Rupert's damaged collarbone would allow. She demanded to taste his cock and sucked it into her mouth as far as it would go, relishing its salty firmness. She even insisted on him forcing his full length into her anus, so she could know what sensations he had felt at the hands of the abusing priest. At the moment Rupert's shaft entered her rectum though, a passing barge on the river sounded a klaxon and, as if a switch had flipped, Holda's excitement switched to embarrassment. She felt humiliated and violated, as though observed by a hundred hidden eyes. Sensing her distress, Rupert held her and kissed her until her body relaxed and responded to his touch once more.

"You're a witchy woman," he murmured in her ear. "You've got me completely in your power."

What a strange thing, thought Holda, that in medieval times, the single thing most likely to draw accusations of witchcraft down on a woman, was being sexually active. Back then the delights of the flesh were seen as fundamentally sinful. But it's such a heavenly experience. How could it possibly be unholy? Rupert's a Catholic, even if he's lapsed. I wonder whether he'll be whispering about this one day to some priest. Will he refer to this wonderful moment as 'fornication' and have to say a few Ave Marias as penance? She was about to open her mouth and ask him a question, but his lips descended on hers and they were immediately locked in another rapturous kiss.

"We still don't have a plan for getting the manuscript!" squealed Holda suddenly when they separated again and lay side by side on the sandy parka.

"How about I create some kind of diversion?" suggested Rupert. "You grab the book, run out to the car with it and drive off. They don't have a vehicle and they won't know where you're taking it. By the time they can call a taxi to follow you, you'll be long gone."

"Where would I go? They'll look for me at the hotel for sure."

"To Father Dietrich's. There has to be a good hiding place at Haus Gripswald. Or better still, you can dismantle the book there and with Father Dietrich's help you can incapacitate it."

"It has to be worth a try," cried Holda. "Come on!"

Chapter 13

The lights were on in Father Jacobi's cottage as they pulled up outside. The first thing they noticed was the priest himself standing on the front doorstep smoking a cigarette.

"I didn't know he smoked," observed Holda.

"He doesn't," said Rupert, puzzled. "I wonder why he's taken it up now."

They got out of the car and approached the house. Jacobi tossed away the lighted stub and a forced smile crossed his face.

"We weren't sure what was keeping you," he blurted out. "Ambrosius, I mean Professor Finster, asked me to keep an eye out for you."

They were afraid we wouldn't return, thought Holda. They have to offer up a virgin to Satan. We need to get the book away from them. But that's not enough because they already know its contents. They might still be able to hold the black Mass without the manuscript. We will have to finesse the timing. I have to get away with the book just ahead of the ceremony, when they can't easily capture a replacement virgin. Then they won't hold the black Mass at all. They can't risk raising Satan if they've nothing to offer him. If we're too early they'll still find a way to make it happen. If we're too late, they'll have raised the devil before I can get away. Who knows what will happen then?

"When did you take up smoking?" asked Rupert insolently.

"I don't normally," replied Jacobi apologetically. Then his voice lowered almost to a growl. "That man is completely insufferable. I can't tell which of them is creating the oppressive atmosphere in the house - the book or him. I had to come outside. The cigarette was just an excuse. I had half a packet lying about which I confiscated last week from a choirboy..." His voice tailed off on the last word as he caught Rupert's expression. The next moment the fist at the end of Rupert's good arm slammed into the side of his face, knocking him sideways against the doorframe.

"You're supposed to be retired," shouted Rupert furiously. "What are you doing still hanging about choirboys, you fucking vile pervert?"

The front door opened and the dark face of Azriel Finster peered out. He smiled with evident relief when he saw Holda and Rupert in front of him, and then his mouth stretched to a satisfied grin as he looked down at the figure of Jacobi sprawling across the doorstep with a trail of blood oozing from one nostril.

"Rupert!" cried Holda, shocked.

"Sorry," he grinned back at her sheepishly. Then, "Not sorry, actually. That felt great."

"Chickens will always come home to roost," observed the professor and Holda wondered whether the remark was directed at Jacobi, or her and Rupert.

"Come into the warm," he continued. "I have just lighted the log burner in the living room. Father Jacobi has an excellent collection of whiskies hidden in the hall cupboard. May I perhaps offer you a drink?"

He stood aside and motioned Holda and Rupert inside, then spoke sharply to the priest.

"Get up off the doorstep, you old fool. You know your tasks. Get on with the final preparations while I speak with my student. Oh, and bring us three tumblers."

Jacobi hauled himself to his feet, pushed past the professor into the hallway and disappeared to the kitchen. Holda, Rupert and the professor headed for the living room where the stove was indeed blasting heat into the tiny room. Jacobi fetched three tumblers from the kitchen and placed them on the desk where a bottle of single malt whisky was set next to the open manuscript. He retreated again quickly to the kitchen. Holda saw that the book was turned to Marieken's first blank page and realised with a shock that there was now no writing to be seen.

"Where's the message gone?" she blurted out.

"That's precisely what I would like to know," replied Azriel, his calm voice failing to conceal his disquiet. "I need to know how that part of the book works."

"But I have no idea!" cried out Holda. "The words just appear from nowhere on the page. I saw them briefly at the windmill and then they materialised properly here while I was working on deciphering Johannes von Deibel's text."

"Was the calligraphy the same as von Deibel's?" demanded Azriel.

"No, no, it was quite different," answered Holda. "I think it must have been Marieken's handwriting. It's written on her skin," she gulped.

Also in my jotter, she realised with a shock. I must have somehow been channelling Marieken when I was transcribing the text. But what does that even mean?

Azriel Finster seated himself in one of the armchairs by the woodstove and stroked his beard thoughtfully.

"I wonder," he brooded, "whether it's just you she wants to talk to. It's a risk of course. You never know what mischief may come of it. I think there is still time for a small experiment. The process was described by one of the esoteric scholars of the fourteenth century, but I've never had an opportunity to try it before."

He stood up and opened the door, calling out to Jacobi in the kitchen.

"Where do you keep your fountain pen, Paulus?"

A muffled reply came from down the hall and Finster strode to the desk, pulled out a drawer and fished out a pen.

"It's a bit dried up," he observed on examining it, "but I think it will do the job."

Then he span around swiftly and grabbed Holda's left wrist in a tight grasp, forcing her hand palm upwards onto the desktop next to the manuscript and the glasses. In the same instant he produced a flick-knife from his pocket and snapped it open. Holda let out a terrified scream as he drove the blade deep into the palm of her hand. Rupert, who was seated on the sofa, leapt to his feet but Finster stopped him with a fierce glare.

"Stay where you are, Keller," he snarled. "This is between Holda and Marieken now. Holda needs to have a proper conversation with the dead girl."

He released his grip on Holda's wrist and she held her hand up. A thick trickle of blood was pulsing from the wound in her hand. Azriel handed her one of the empty whisky tumblers.

"Catch the blood," he hissed harshly. "Don't waste it or I'll have to cut you again."

Shaking now with shock and only with difficulty holding back sobs, Holda held up the tumbler and let the sticky, red liquid ooze into the bottom of the glass.

"Hold it down, you need to produce more than that," growled Azriel. "That's more like it," he added as Holda dropped her bleeding hand earthwards and the blood flowed more freely. "I think that's going to be enough." He handed her the fountain pen.

"I want you to write to Marieken," he ordered. "Get her to answer you."

"I can't write in this book using my blood," cried Holda in horror. "It will capture my soul. I'll spend eternity stuck in limbo with Johannes von Deibel."

"That's superstitious nonsense," replied Azriel coldly. "Even if it weren't, every scholar of medieval manuscripts knows perfectly well how to clean fresh blood off old documents. Vellum's even easier than paper as it doesn't distort. Of course we won't leave your stupid scrawls on the page. I despair of the quality of graduate students they send me these days. Now, sit down dammit and ask Marieken a question. We don't have much time. I'll stand over here in the doorway. She obviously doesn't want to speak to the likes of me."

We don't have much time, do we? thought Holda. That mean the planets must align soon. We still have to get the book and get away. She glanced across at Rupert who was now sitting on the edge of the sofa watching the proceedings intently, then at Azriel whose frame blocked the only exit from the room.

Holda dipped the nib of the ink into the glass of blood, and held it hovering above the page.

Do I dare to write on the page? she thought anxiously. He says it can be cleaned off, but I don't think

I trust him. What would I write anyway? This is worse than trying to write a thesis plan. I can't have writer's block now.

Her hand shook and a splash of blood dropped onto the page. Holda screamed. A derisory snort came from the doorway and Holda flushed with silent rage. Azriel had better be right about erasing blood, she thought, her eyes pricking with tears. Well, here goes.

She placed the nib on the page and wrote: Segg mich wo du heesst?

"I've written 'tell me what you are called' in medieval Rhineland German," she explained aloud, both for Rupert's benefit and to try to steady her own nerves.

For a long moment she thought the experiment had failed. Then gradually, faint words appeared on the tan skin just below Holda's question. Over the space of five or six seconds they darkened just enough to be legible:

Marieken von Pesch. Bitte, kom mich ze helf.

"Oh my God," breathed Holda. "It's working. I'm actually talking to Marieken."

Rupert leapt to his feet and stood behind Holda's chair. Azriel, over near the door, was observing the whole procedure intently.

"Ask her how we can help her," suggested Rupert.

Holda picked up her pen again and phrased the question. The answer came back swiftly this time: Burn the book. Now. Do not wait.

Holda dipped the nib into the glass of blood again and wrote: What will happen to you and Wil?

There was a pause which lasted for so long that Holda thought no answer was coming. Then more words appeared: No matter. It must be done. Save the world. Satan must not rise again.

"No," cried Holda. "Don't give up Marieken. Never, ever give up."

She was about to dip her pen back into the blood but Rupert caught her wrist with his good hand.

"Be careful," he whispered. His eyes flicked in the direction of the door and back to Holda, who took a deep breath and wrote one more word on the page: Amen.

"That's enough," Azriel Finster's voice snapped out across the room. "An interesting experiment, Holda, but more of a diversion than a revelation. He strode across to the desk, poured out a measure of whisky into each of the remaining clean glasses and handed one each to Rupert and Holda.

"Drink this while I get a bandage for that hand of yours," he ordered. "And some ice to remove the blood from the vellum. It has to be done while the stain is fresh. If it dries and goes brown you can't remove it. Ever. You did know that, didn't you Holda?"

"No, I didn't," squeaked Holda, with rising panic in her voice. "I've never bled on a manuscript before. Please hurry Azriel. I'm scared."

Azriel strode out of the living room towards the kitchen. Rupert put his arm around Holda and chinked his glass against hers.

"You darling, brave girl," he comforted her. "Hang on in there."

He drained his glass and Holda followed suit. The spirit seared its way to her stomach, but its warmth afforded no comfort. "Rupert, I'm terrified. What's going to happen now? Oh God, I'm so frightened I think I'm going to faint."

Rupert steered her quickly to the sofa. "You've lost quite a lot of blood," he fretted. "Let me staunch that cut for you until Azriel brings the bandage."

A few moments later when Azriel Finster returned from the kitchen empty handed, he found Holda and Rupert slumped on the sofa, both snoring sonorously. He chuckled softly to himself and walked over to the desk where the book was still open. Holda's questions were still plainly visible on the tan page in a dullish red, but Marieken's answers had vanished. Checking that the writing was dry, Professor Finster closed the book and carried it out of the room in the manner of a tray, with the two empty whisky glasses and the tumbler smeared with congealed blood on top.

Half an hour later he came back, this time together with Father Jacobi who was carrying a shoebox full of brownish coloured candles and other items.

"Are you sure they'll stay asleep until we start?" asked the priest nervously.

"What do you take me for?" snapped Azriel back. "Those drops could knock out a horse. They wouldn't wake up if a herd of cows stampeded through the room."

Jacobi smirked and, approaching the sleeping figures, aimed a vicious kick at Rupert's shin. Rupert grunted but slept on.

"Get the desk set up as the altar like I told you," barked Finster. "Don't light the candles yet. Take special care drawing the symbols. Wait, I'll get the book and you can copy them out."

He went back to the kitchen and returned with the manuscript. He placed it open on the desk at one of the Latin pages, then turned back to the sleeping couple on the sofa.

"It was a piece of luck having this dainty little morsel turn up in my faculty at Cambridge," he murmured to himself with a chuckle. "There are not many language students who are still virgins by the time they graduate. Well Holda, tonight you will lose your virginity in style."

He pulled Rupert off the sofa and let him slump unconscious onto the floor. Then he began to undress the sleeping girl. It was harder work than he had expected as her body was a resistant, dead weight. He had broken into a sweat by the time he had managed to peel the tight jeans and panties from her.

"You could have cut the clothes off," observed Jacobi dryly as he approached and daubed pentagrams on Holda's bare breasts in some black, viscous fluid which he held in a jar. "I do that sometimes with miscreants."

"When I want your advice I'll ask for it," retorted Azriel. "Help me carry the girl."

Between them they hauled the limp form of Holda off the sofa and dragged her to the desk. Finster positioned her, slumped face down across the top. He fished into the shoebox and pulled out a set of black leather straps. "These are proper heirlooms," he chuckled more to himself than to Jacobi. "These have been passed down in our family for at least five generations." He tied one strap tightly around Holda's wrists and secured it to the window catch behind the desk. The other two he slipped around her ankles and tightened them around the front legs of the desk so that she was spread-eagled. Jacobi positioned candles on either side of her head. Finster ran his hand lasciviously over Holda's naked buttocks.

"It's tragic that Johannes von Deibel's theory turned out to be false," he whispered softly. "Just imagine if Satan were to possess my body and let me be the one to impregnate this gorgeous little bitch."

He checked his wristwatch.

"You may light the candles now, Paulus," he declared. "It is time."

The candles burned with a smoky, dull flame. Azriel caught up the manuscript and turned to one of the Latin pages. In a resolute voice he began to read out loud. At the same time, Jacobi uncorked a fat bottle and waved it close to Holda's face. Her eyelids flickered and opened. Then she began to shriek.

Finster's voice was still pronouncing his incantation. He reached the end of it and there was silence for a moment. Then a terrible scream erupted from Azriel's lips. When he next spoke his voice had altered terribly. It was deep, thunderous and menacing. The whole house shook and a pane of the window to which Holda was restrained cracked across the middle.

"For what have I been summoned?" boomed the voice.

Jacobi was gawping in astonished terror at the figure of Professor Finster, whose face was suddenly suffused, choleric, enraged. His eyes were bursting from their sockets and the veins on his forehead and neck stood out fiercely.

"We have brought you a virgin, Master," squeaked Jacobi, dropping the bottle he was holding, which rolled across the carpet towards the slumped figure of Rupert Keller. "We fetched her so that you might conceive our lord, the anti-Christ."

In a frenzy, the arms of Azriel Finster stretched out towards Holda, grabbed her by the wrists and ripped her away from the desk. The restraints held for a moment, then snapped, leaving dark wheals on her wrists and ankles where they had been. Finster hurled her to the sofa, next to which Rupert's figure was beginning to stir.

"Fools," bellowed the hideous voice that was not Azriel Finster's. "Know that Lord Satan rises in his own form only if there is a true virgin awaiting him. That creature is not undefiled. There is but one orifice in this room which is as yet unpenetrated and that lies between the fool Jacobi's buttocks. That one my loyal servant Azriel's cock shall take."

The figure seized hold of Father Jacobi and hurled him so hard across the desk that he screamed out in terror and pain. A second later the trousers and underwear were brutally ripped from his flabby body and the erect penis of Azriel Finster was thrusting violently into his anus. Father Jacobi's howls became higher and shriller with every thrust. His legs kicked furiously but struck only empty air. Eventually his head was thrown back in a long, loud, wail of agony. Holda and Rupert watched in horror as something steel glinted in the hand of Azriel Finster. A high pitched gurgling sound followed and Azriel's knife dropped onto the desktop, together with something red and bloody.

"Oh God, his tongue. It's his tongue!" screamed Holda.

Rupert clapped his hand over her mouth. "Keep quiet," he hissed.

As Azriel stepped backwards, his posture changed suddenly. For a second he stood upright, then his body seemed to sag into itself and he collapsed in a heap on the floor. Jacobi was still howling; a high pitched, wordless wail. Then he hauled himself to his feet and clapped his hands to his face. Blood spurted between his fingers and down over his naked legs. Still bellowing, Jacobi made a dash for the door, ran down the hall and out of the house.

Rupert struggled to his feet and held Holda tightly for a moment, then he went over and examined the figure of Azriel Finster. He knelt down and felt the side of the man's neck with two fingers.

"He's in cardiac arrest. I think he's dead," he gasped.

"Do not resuscitate him," hissed Holda. "Under no circumstances. Pass me my clothes."

She dressed quickly and grabbed the book from the desk, tucking it under her coat.

"Which way do you think Jacobi went?" she asked.

Rupert ran out into the hall.

"If you want to find him, it won't be difficult," he called. "We can follow the trail of blood."

Sure enough there was a distinct track of red splatters all down the hall, out of the garden gate and up onto the dyke path.

"We'd better follow him," shouted Rupert. "He was badly injured. Whatever we think of the old devil, we can't leave him like that."

They tracked the trail of blood along the top of the dyke.

"He's heading for Gisela's bench," gasped Holda. "Look, there he is."

A shaft of moonlight had emerged from behind a cloud and the figure of Father Jacobi was stumbling along the path. Suddenly he turned and half ran, half fell down the bank to the water's edge.

"Father, what are you doing?" screamed Holda in alarm. "Come back. We're here to save you."

They ran to where the priest had vanished down the bank.

"Father Jacobi!" shrieked Holda.

There was an answering howl of despair from somewhere down in the river, followed by a splashing sound and then silence.

Chapter 14

It was late next morning when Holda and Rupert drew up in the little black Volkswagen outside the grand portal of Haus Gripswald. The pair had spent nearly all night trying every method they could think of to remove Holda's writing from the page at the back of the manuscript. Ice, water, detergent, even bleach had all proved ineffective. It was an exhausted, subdued and tearful Holda who had driven down and checked out of her hotel for good that morning, then returned with her luggage to Rupert's flat. After that, she had unpicked the stitching on the book's spine, eased away the covering from the boards and teased the different pages free. She had divided the components appropriately into three large manila envelopes which she labelled with a fat black marker: 'Marieken', 'Wil' and 'The evil fucking bastard'.

Rupert was still sporting a sling. As they got out of the car and went to open the hatchback, Rupert hugged Holda tightly and told her everything would turn out fine. But his hollow eyes and lined forehead told a different story.

Father Dietrich's aged face creased into a smile when he saw the two companions enter his room safely. His grin widened still further as he spotted that they were carrying three pouches. He did wag an arthritic warning finger at them both when he saw the inscription on Johannes von Deibel's package, though his face betrayed amusement.

"Come and sit down and tell me all about it," he wheezed. "Sister Barbara has kept the radio hidden from me all morning. She only does that when there's something terrible she is trying to keep from me. She thinks my heart is too frail to hear bad news. I feared something diabolical had happened to you. I have prayed for you half the night, my children."

"The news is full of what they speculate to be a murder-suicide with a deviant sexual motive," replied Rupert. "The half-naked body of Holda's professor was found in Father Jacobi's living room, and Father Jacobi's corpse was fished out of the Rhine at Uerdingen late last night. What the broadcasts don't mention is that he left his tongue behind when he went into the river. The police must be keeping that detail to themselves. Actually, the press have got just about every aspect of the story wrong, so you might as well ignore them and hear what really happened straight from the horse's mouth."

At this point, Sister Barbara came in carrying a tray with coffee and an aromatic, thick honey cake. When she had left the room again, they sat together while Holda and Rupert, speaking quickly and urgently, recounted their story. The old priest shook his head and clicked his tongue as the pair attempted at first to gloss over the issue of Holda's lost virginity.

"Tell me everything, exactly as it happened," he insisted. "Remember, a priest has heard more of this kind of technicality than you can possibly imagine. It is not as though you are speaking with your own grandfather."

When they got to the part where Holda had written in the book in her own blood, his face became grave and thoughtful.

"That's the thing we're so scared of, Father," she blurted out. "We tried to clean it off with ice and cold water like Azriel said. We even looked up ways of cleaning blood off manuscripts on the Internet, but nothing worked. You can still see my writing on Marieken's first page."

"I do not suppose the book's curse really does extend to you. But let us try to ensure your safety a different way," suggested Father Dietrich slowly. "What I propose to do is read the absolution of the dead over Wil and Marieken's envelopes. I will, at the same time, include your name and ask that your soul is presented to God for forgiveness. If it works, your blood will join with Wil and Marieken's remains in my coffin when I am buried. I am confident that will be enough to ensure your safety." Then he leaned forward and grasped Holda's hand urgently.

"Join the Catholic church, child. Ask for baptism and confirmation. Or, if you must, join another religion, for all are paths to God. Repent and pray. Do not remain distant from the lord. You must rely on Him to save your soul."

Holda squeezed his hand in acknowledgement of his concern, but then pulled it away.

I have free will, she thought fiercely. I'm the only one who can decide what to believe and how to live. God only has rules and restrictions to offer. His promises of Paradise versus Hell are entwined in rules to control my life. I love Rupert, but Father Dietrich would call our beautiful love 'sinful fornication' because we're not married. I'm not a strong virgin any more, I'm a mighty woman. I'm no longer just the ghost of a human being, I'm solid. But how could I be real if I never cast a shadow? I need my darker side in order to be whole. It's nobody else's business whether I'm a virgin. Not his, not the church's and not Azriel's. It's only Satan and the Catholic church who are obsessed with fornication and virginity, without recognising the beauty and love that belongs with it. It was their representative, Father Jacobi, the fallen priest, who raped choirboys. They all use sex, or lack of it, as a means of asserting control over others' lives. I want nothing more to do with any of that.

"Father," she answered, "let's focus on saving Marieken and Wil."

She placed the two envelopes containing the mortal remains of those two fourteenth century figures onto Father Dietrich's lap.

"We will deal with Johannes von Deibel first," answered the priest. "Holda, please would you throw his envelope into the fireplace?"

Holda was only too happy to comply. She rose and carried the brown manila package across to the large, sandstone fireplace on the other side of the room where a log fire was alight.

"This is for Marieken and Wil," she declared forcefully, "and all the other people you harmed in your lifetime."

She tossed the pouch into the fire. The package landed for a moment, balanced against a log and silhouetted against the glowing embers. Then a bluish flame began to lick round the envelope and a sound like a long, shrill scream emitted from the hearth.

"It's just gas escaping from one of the logs," stated Father Dietrich firmly as Holda shrieked, ran back and clutched Rupert in alarm.

"The hell it is," muttered Rupert.

"Let's call it that for now," hissed Holda back. "The sooner we get away from every part of this book the better."

Sister Barbara knocked once and entered.

"I thought I heard someone call," she queried. "Is anything the matter?"

"Everything is as it should be," replied Father Dietrich. "But I need you to call Father Peters on the telephone at once. I wish to say a requiem Mass for three people this evening. I would like to borrow his chapel in Ossum village for the purpose. I will also need him and one of his strong parishioners to come here and carry me down the stairs. It will preferably be someone with a large car, big enough to fit my wheelchair in the back to transport me there. Tell him I will explain everything when he gets here."

"What on earth...?" began Sister Barbara, but catching the priest's look she broke off and moved back to the door, shaking her head as she went.

"She is used to my occasional eccentricities," chuckled Father Dietrich. "Some days she is convinced dementia has finally claimed me."

Sister Barbara returned shortly afterwards with news that the old priest would be picked up at six thirty by Father Peters and the owner of Bungard's riding school.

"The wheelchair will have to ride in the horsebox," shouted Sister Barbara disapprovingly in her stentorious voice. "Herr Bungard asks that you don't put any corpses in his horse-carrier."

"The deceased will travel with me in the full dignity of my breast pocket," replied Father Dietrich with a chuckle which ended in a coughing fit.

Sister Barbara raised an eyebrow.

"Completely unhinged," she muttered under her breath. "I shall have to call the doctor out later if he carries on like this." Then she addressed Rupert and Holda, also using the tone she reserved for the hard of comprehension.

"It's time for the father's nap now. He gets very tired, you know. I shall have to ask you to return another time."

"Come to the Mass," wheezed Father Dietrich. "Half past six at Ossum chapel."

"We'll be there," promised Holda.

She and Rupert descended the staircase and drove away towards Büderich and Rupert's flat.

They had two hours to spare before they needed to set off again for Ossum. Rupert and Holda spent the first hour making love in Rupert's wide, comfortable bed. When they finished, they went for a shower together and Holda dressed in the most sombre clothes she owned. Rupert put on black jeans, black shoes and a dark blue shirt. Then, while Holda put the kettle on for tea, Rupert sat down at his computer to check his email.

"Hello!" he exclaimed a moment later. "There's a message with an attachment from the Düsseldorf archive. Remember they said they'd email me a scan of their court records from 1361? Well, they've sent it. Of course it's too late now; the book is destroyed anyway. There never will be an exhibition."

Holda brought over two steaming mugs.

"Let's take a look anyway," she replied. "We've got a bit of time to spare before we have to leave."

"Rupert clicked open the attachment and a scan of an old, handwritten book filled the screen."

"I can't make head or tail of it," he lamented, obviously disappointed.

"Make way for the medievalist," replied Holda. "Or maybe ex-medievalist. I don't suppose I'll ever manage to complete my doctorate after all that's happened. After all this, I don't know whether I could touch a medieval manuscript again."

Rupert moved so that Holda could sit in front of his computer screen. She scrolled slowly down the page.

"It looks like there was a crime wave of sheep stealing and drunkenness in the fourteenth century Rhineland," she chuckled, then suddenly let out a gasp. "Oh, but wait. Here's poor old Wil Biskup. Look."

She read out a single sentence recording that one Willem Biskup of Ossum had been found guilty of the violation and murder of Marieken von Pesch in May 1361, and was sentenced to hang.

They were silent for a moment.

"Back then, people who were hanged weren't given a Christian burial," sighed Rupert. "They were often buried at a crossroads or on the heath. They weren't permitted to lie in hallowed ground."

"But Willem wasn't a murderer or a rapist," protested Holda. "He deserves his proper funeral this evening, just as Marieken does."

She scrolled on a little further and then gave a little squeak.

"How odd," she cried out. "Look at this Rupert. There was a witch trial in November that same year. Three people were hanged for witchcraft. I do hope they were some of the ones who were at von Deibel's black Mass. It's written here. 'On this day 14th of November 1361 were found guilty of the black arts and adoration of the enemy Satan three deplorables of the village of Bishke: Klaus Bruynswyk, Felix Möbius, and Lisken Finster. They are sentenced to hang.'"

"Felix Möbius!" exclaimed Rupert. "That's the same name as our mayor's husband."

"And Lisken Finster," whispered Holda. "I wonder... didn't you say that Azriel found out about the book because he was related to the mayor?"

"It must be a coincidence," whispered Rupert. "Mustn't it?"

"I could still ask Marieken," suggested Holda. "She might know."

"You'll do no such thing," hissed Rupert firmly. "There's to be no more messing about with bloody writing on those pages. Come on. We can't be late for the funeral."

On the drive up to Ossum they spoke of other, happier things. They discovered a shared taste for renaissance music and Italian food, and a mutual dislike of hip hop, beetroot and Brussels sprouts. Neither had ever been skiing. Both liked walking and reading. Most importantly, both loved the other with the fascination of a newly found obsession.

At Ossum they found the old priest being manoeuvred into his wheelchair, at the door of the little, old, brick chapel. Holda helped as they hauled him up the chapel steps. Rupert watched helplessly as his arm was still in a sling. They placed Father Dietrich's wheelchair in front of the altar with the two envelopes before him on a small trestle, decorated with a white altar cloth. Then the voice of the old priest rose and he began to sing the Introit in a quavering but practiced voice. Father Peters and the owner of the horsebox joined in with responses. Holda felt like an interloper until she remembered that her soul too was included in the ceremony.

I must be the only person who ever turned up alive at their own funeral, she thought. I'd say it was the weirdest thing that ever happened to me except that, after the past few days, I'm sure that's not true. How odd. I was still so frightened about being trapped in the manuscript when I came into the chapel. But now, for the first time in ages, I can sense happy, safe and positive vibes about the future. I feel as though I'm free of the book, released from Azriel's influence and rid of Jacobi the stalker. I've met Rupert and right now I believe he's the one. How bizarre that I'm sitting here at a requiem Mass feeling elated. It's as though a pendulum has swung in the other direction, now that the book that was sapping my happiness has been burnt. She ducked her head down and tried to restrain the ecstatic smile which kept breaking out spontaneously across her features.

The old priest's voice had moved to a spoken part of the service but Holda had stopped concentrating on the words. She was lost in thought now.

But where do I go next? Back to Cambridge? They must find me another supervisor. Azriel's chair won't be empty for long. It will give me time to get my thesis back on track. What about Rupert? He'll probably want to stay here and build up his archive. Maybe there's a medieval German department in Düsseldorf or Duisburg University. Even commuting from here as far as Cologne or Aachen might be possible if I didn't have to teach there every day. When probate comes through from my parents' estate, I'll have the money to bridge any gap. I must discuss it all with Rupert when the time feels right.

As the ceremony progressed, the remembrance of her parents' funeral came flooding back to her, but even that reflection now lacked the power to sadden her.

I must tidy up all the loose ends though, she mused. I must take their ashes and scatter them by the ruins in Delos as they requested. I must sell the house and all their things. I must start again as me this time.

The requiem Mass was nearly at an end and Father Dietrich was pronouncing the absolution of the dead over the two manila envelopes. She heard her own name mentioned. Father Dietrich beckoned her forward and, as she knelt before him, he laid a hand on her head and pronounced absolution and a blessing over her.

I hope it works. If it doesn't, I don't suppose his prayers can do any harm, she thought. It makes him feel like he's done something good. At least he'll be able to die in peace now.

Chapter 15

It was a month later that Holda and Rupert's plane landed at the little airport on Mykonos for their first holiday together. Rupert's arm was completely healed and he was keen to swim in the sea to build up strength in it again. In the first few days they swam and lounged on the beach during the day, and walked into town at sunset to explore the local fish restaurants and relish the tannin-rich local wines in the evenings. They explored the island together and marvelled at everything they found, from beautiful views and buildings, to geckoes and butterflies, to the pelican which once flapped onto the balcony of the restaurant they were eating at. Everything was a new, special, treasured memory to be stored away and hoarded, because it was the first time they had done any of these things together.

On the fifth day Holda fished the urn with her parents' ashes out of her suitcase and shoved it into her backpack. She and Rupert caught the early ferry across to the island of Delos and spent two hours walking in the sunshine around the ancient ruins there. They strolled up the avenue flanked by great stone lions to the sanctuary of Apollo, where Holda took out the urn from her rucksack.

"Vale Mater, vale Pater," she whispered. Then she began slowly to spread the contents of the urn around the dusty grounds of the temple.

When they returned to Meerbusch, the local newspaper was running a full page obituary of the town's oldest resident, the retired priest, Father Dietrich. A death notice invited all his friends and former parishioners to attend the Mass that Friday, which was to be held in the main church in Büderich owing to the large number of attendees expected.

Holda and Rupert attended the requiem, though they hovered shyly at the back of the church. It was standing room only. They nodded to Sister Barbara who was up front in the choir, but she did not appear to recognise them. Father Peters shook their hands warmly at the church door afterwards and thanked them for coming.

"I won't ever forget that Mass at the Ossum chapel," he reflected. "What a strange thing that was. And he had an odd request about those envelopes towards the end too. He insisted we place those two pouches in the casket with him. Sister Barbara was most put out, but she did do it. I checked before the coffin lid was closed. I'm still completely in the dark about the whole affair. I have to confess, I had a look inside the envelopes. One contained a piece of old, dark brown leather and the other some light brown rectangular pages of vellum with nothing written on them."

"Nothing at all?" asked Holda, startled. She held her breath until the answer came.

"No, they looked like they'd come out of some ancient book, but they'd obviously never been written on. I wonder what it all meant."

Maybe Father Dietrich's idea really worked, thought Holda in amazement. Could it be that my blood was cleansed from the pages by his prayers?

"Perhaps Sister Barbara was right after all," the priest continued. "She did say he'd started behaving oddly towards the end."

Father Peters fished in his pocket and handed Holda a thick, white envelope.

"Talking of envelopes, before he died, Father Dietrich asked me to give this to you. I promise you I haven't looked in this one," he added with an embarrassed smile. "It's still sealed."

Holda looked puzzled.

"For me? I wonder what that can be. Thank you very much, Father," she replied as the priest released her palm from his firm valedictory grip.

"You are welcome my child. Now, I really must be off or I'll be late for the cemetery. Will you come to the committal? Technically it's family and his carers only, but I'm sure you'd be made welcome."

"Oh no, we couldn't. We only got to know Father Dietrich in the past few weeks. We wouldn't like to intrude on a private family burial," answered Rupert, also shaking the priest's hand.

Later, back at Rupert's flat, Holda sat down on the sofa and slit open the envelope with her thumbnail. A familiar yellow document fell out, with an accompanying note in a shaky and barely legible handwriting. Holda managed to decipher it only with difficulty:

Dear Holda,

If you are reading this note, know that I am finally at peace along with Marieken von Pesch and Wil Biskup. Following our requiem Mass in the chapel at Ossum, no further traces of your blood were to be found on any of the pages from the manuscript. I take this as a sure sign that you are released from that curse. In his mercy our saviour has delivered you for now. I pray you will continue to walk with God in the future. Do not turn your back on Him. Remember that Lucifer's crime was to seek independence from God.

I am sending you the letter and confession of Heinrich Plenkers as a keepsake and reminder of how he saved his soul from the inferno. Keep it safe, my child. Read it whenever you need a reminder of God's mercy and, whatever you do, do not give it to that young man of yours for his archive.

May the blessing of our lord be upon you now and forever.

Dietrich

His signature was followed by the sign of the cross.

Holda read the letter aloud to Rupert who had joined her on the couch. He eyed the yellow parchment regretfully.

"It's such a shame," he moaned. "An exhibition solving the grisly, two hundred year old murders in the chapel of Schloss Pesch would be a sensation. We'd earn a fortune for the town council. The newspapers would have a field day. We might even get national television coverage."

"Rupert," scolded Holda fiercely, "stop it. You can't reveal the secrets of the confessional. No wonder Father Dietrich left the letter to me, not you."

"Well, after you burned the only really valuable manuscript we ever had in our archives, surely you could see your way to donating one little letter," argued Rupert. "I could have lost my job over you destroying that book."

"So long as the mayor still thinks it was lost in the tornado," retorted Holda, "there's no need for us to say anything more about it."

He's forgotten that I still have photographs of the entire document on my laptop, she thought to herself. I really must delete them tonight. We've seen the kind of harm that manuscript can do. It's a tragedy for academia but those images must not be seen by anybody ever again.

"Rupert, I'm sort of wondering what to do now. I ought to return to Cambridge and get on with my doctorate. But I'm getting quite attached to the Rhineland, now that I've met you. I did wonder whether I might transfer to Düsseldorf University and stick around here. What do you think?"

Rupert threw his arms around her and pulled her close to him.

"I'd like nothing better. Do you really mean it? Do you think you could face sharing an apartment with a town archivist?"

"Certainly not," protested Holda in mock indignation. Then, kissing his frowning forehead, she added, "I'll put my parents' place on the market and with the proceeds we'll be able to buy a house together. We won't need to squeeze into your apartment any more. We'll buy something with a great big study for each of us, and a garden. I hear the soil is brilliant here on the Rhine plain. We'll have an orchard with a swing and a vegetable patch and masses of flowers."

It was two months later that Rupert came home from work with a strangely troubled expression on his face. He was carrying a large cardboard box.

"The archive's been given some new material," he announced. "The church finally got permission to clear out Father Jacobi's old house now that the police and the coroner have finished with it. They've given us a pile of documents to look through. It looks like they're mainly letters and diaries. I don't know if I want to look at Jacobi's diaries personally." He paused.

Holda hugged him and then kept her arms encircled around him. She could sense the tension in his body as he silently battled the tide of rising memories.

"I'll give you a hand with it if you like," she offered reassuringly. "Or, I'll even do all of it for you. I've got time on my hands. I don't start at Düsseldorf University for another month.

It took two days until she found the letter, tucked into a tatty jotter full of strange coded scribbles.

Dear Paul,

I can't believe you're still ignoring me after everything you've done. You were the one who kept nagging for me to go the whole way. Then, ever since you got me drunk and we did have sex, you've been pretending not to be interested any more. I know you love me really underneath it all though. I feel we're destined to spend our lives together. Do you know how I know? Because I have some exciting news for you. Paul, you're going to be a father. Yes, really. I was at the doctor's this morning and he confirmed that I'm having a baby. Our baby, Paul. Just think of that. Now you'll have to give up this silly idea about becoming a priest. We'll get married and we'll have a wonderful family together. Paul, please do come tonight to our place by the river. We can talk about it all and then go and break the news to your parents and my father. I'm so excited I can hardly wait until I see you.

All my love and a thousand million kisses, from your loving Gisela

"Let me see," cried Rupert after Holda had read the letter aloud. He scanned it then slumped heavily down onto the sofa and stared at her gravely. "The letter is dated 2nd May 1959, the same day that Gisela drowned."

"Could Jacobi have made a diary entry for that day?" wondered Holda. "I've only found the more recent ones so far and they're mostly written in some cryptic code." She reached into the cardboard box and began pulling out old exercise books by the dozen. This time Rupert helped her sort through them.

"I've found it," he announced at last. He read aloud:

"May 2nd 1959. G wrote to me again and not just her normal drivel. She claims she has a bun in the oven. I met her at the usual place. We had sex again. Missionary and doggy. While she was washing herself off at the edge of the water, I shoved her in the Rhine and held her under. When she went limp I pushed her out into the current. Got home and managed to dry my clothes without anyone seeing. Success."

"So that's why Father Dietrich wouldn't give him absolution!" cried Holda. "He was a murderer and he wasn't the slightest bit repentant either. Does Hell even have a pit hot enough for him and Johannes von Deibel?"

"I really hope it does," spat out Rupert. His face was furious. "Holda, we need to burn these diaries. Gisela is dead and so is Jacobi. But lots of his victims are alive and still living here. Nobody wants strangers reading accounts of them being abused as children, especially not written by the rapist himself. Put everything back in the box and we'll take it straight down to the Rhine and have a bonfire on the beach."

"I think that's a very good idea," replied Holda as she began to pack the box.

Epilogue

It was spring again when Holda and Rupert finally moved into their newly renovated house in the old part of Lank-Latum. They had chosen every part of the decoration and furnishings together, with the exception of the two studies. These rooms each of the pair had stamped with their own personality. Rupert's was stuffed with recording gear, computer screens and cameras, all neatly labelled and stored in sleek cupboards. Holda's was lined with bookshelves and, even on this first day, her desk was already strewn with papers, notepads and books. The whole day had been spent unpacking boxes, building furniture and putting up shelves.

"I can't face going to the supermarket for food now," grumbled Holda when late afternoon came around and they sank, exhausted, onto their newly installed couch. "Let's treat ourselves and eat out this evening. We can take the ferry over the Kaiserswerth to that lovely place on the opposite bank of the Rhine. I want to show you something on the way."

"Great idea," replied Rupert. "I'll even pay for dinner, if you like." He grinned impishly. "It's only fair as you paid for the house."

Holda laughed and hit him over the head with a cushion in pretend outrage. But she grabbed her backpack and parka and followed him out to the car all the same.

The crossing between Meerbusch and Kaiserswerth is served by a single flat barge which ploughs its way from one side of the Rhine to the other, ferrying cars, cyclists and pedestrians to and fro. When Holda and Rupert parked up where the road appears to drive straight into the river, they could see the ferryboat setting off from the opposite shore. They watched the vessel chug slowly across the river towards them, apparently aiming a little too far upstream, but then letting the fast flowing current propel it expertly to its correct mooring. A ramp was lowered and the vehicles drove off the ferry and away, up the road towards Meerbusch. Holda and Rupert walked onto the barge as foot passengers and stood looking over the railing when the vessel pulled away from the shore.

Now, thought Holda.

"Rupert," she announced, "here's what I wanted you to see."

She pulled off her backpack, unzipped it and reached inside. She drew out her laptop.

"I still have the photos of Johannes von Deibel's manuscript on here," she stated in a quiet, slightly strained voice.

Rupert gasped. "Of course you do. I'd completely forgotten about that. Holda, do you realise what this means? We can still hold the exhibition after all. We can blow up the images and have them printed on display boards. We can make all those exhibits about spells and potions and the astronomical models after all. We'll put Meerbusch on the map. Oh Holda, this is going to be brilliant!"

"I thought you might say that," sighed Holda. With one deft movement, she hurled the laptop as far as she could into the Rhine. There was a splash and it vanished from view.

"Holda, what the hell?" screamed Rupert.

The churning wash from the ferry intercepted the expanding ripples where the laptop had vanished and erased them completely. In a moment there was nothing visible to mark the spot where the device had disappeared.

"I had to do it, Rupert," she pleaded. "You know as well as I do what evil that book can do. I knew you'd remember the images one day and want to resurrect your exhibition. Rupert, it's over. It can't be done now. This whole story is buried forever. Remember what Father Dietrich said: some stories must be left untold. This one is at the top of that list."

Rupert looked crestfallen but by the time the ferry drew up at the opposite bank of the river he was already coming to terms with his disappointment. He kissed her long and hard by way of apology.

"You're right, of course. I know that," he admitted grudgingly as they disembarked. "It just feels as though every story anyone would be interested in, can't be told - von Deibel's diary, Heinrich Plenkers' confession, Father Jacobi's diaries, even the Nazi mural in the town hall. Right now my role as an archivist seems to be all about suppressing history rather than preserving it. But I admit, I do see how it is safer your way."

"If the real story of the manuscript had ever come out, imagine what harm it could have done in the world," commented Holda, perhaps just a little too sternly. "Look what happened to Henrietta and Heinrich Plenkers. And even hiding it for centuries in the wall of a disused chapel wasn't enough. It still found a way to escape, witch marks notwithstanding. The book itself was malevolent; von Deibel was exerting his evil from beyond the grave. Remember how Azriel and Father Jacobi died horribly when they tried to follow its instructions and got it wrong? You and I only narrowly escaped an unspeakable fate. Rupert, I had to make sure nobody could ever get hold of Johannes von Deibel's missal again. No exhibition or academic paper could be worth the risk of letting anyone try to summon Satan."

She zipped up her now empty backpack and slung it over one shoulder.

Does he suspect anything? she wondered. The physical book was burned. That was where the souls were trapped, including mine. Surely digitised images can't exert any evil influence. I'll hide the computer hard drive in a safe place and nobody will ever find out that I have it. But it is strange that I couldn't make myself destroy those pictures. Every time I tried to erase the files, my finger just wouldn't press the delete key.

She turned away from him and began to walk up the road leading from the river. Rupert watched her with a puzzled gaze for a few moments, then jogged after her and caught her up.

"Come on. I'll race you. I can already see the beer garden from here," he grinned as he drew alongside. "Afterwards we can walk up to the old monastery of St. Suitbert. I wouldn't mind trying to work out where the latrines used to be."

FINIS

About the Author

Cathy Dobson was born in 1963 in Marple, Cheshire, the town after which Agatha Christie named her famous female sleuth, Miss Marple. She studied modern and medieval languages at Cambridge University between 1982–1986. In 1991 she moved to Germany and in 1995 settled in Meerbusch in the Rhineland with her husband, three children and a fluctuating number of cats. Her first novel, *Planet Germany*, was published in 2007, to wide acclaim in the German and British press. *The Devil's Missal* is her second novel.

CPSIA information can be obtained
at www.ICGtesting.com
Printed in the USA
BVHW031717220719
554055BV00015B/1848/P